Brennan and Dr. Wu removed the skeleton from the body bag.

With the container out of the way and the remains laid out on the table, Brennan did a cursory exam. She looked at Dr. Wu. The other woman had seen the same things Brennan had—it was in her eyes.

"Booth," Brennan said. "This is not a hoax. Or anyway, if it's a prank, it's a very expensive one."

"You're sure?"

"For one thing, these bones are not plastic—I can tell you that. They are very much the real thing."

"You can tell already? Is it Musetti? . . . Sorry. I know that's impossible. . . ."

She raised an eyebrow. "Actually not impossible."

"Yeah?"

"Usually, I would need some sort of reference material from the victim to positively ID him . . . but in this case I can tell you this skeleton is definitely *not* Stewart Musetti. Or, more accurately, I can tell you it's not *all* Stewart Musetti."

"Obviously," Booth said. "Last time I saw the guy, he had a lot more skin and hair and, uh, meat on his bones."

Brennan shook her head. "You don't understand."

"I don't?"

"This skeleton is not made up of the body of just one person."

BONES™
BURIED DEEP

MAX ALLAN COLLINS
FEATURING THE CHARACTER CREATED BY
KATHY REICHS

arrow books

Published in the United Kingdom by Arrow Books in 2006

3 5 7 9 10 8 6 4

™ and copyright © 2006 by Twentieth Century Fox Film Corporation.
All Rights Reserved

Arrow Books
The Random House Group Limited
20 Vauxhall Bridge Road, London SW1V 2SA

Random House Australia (Pty) Limited
20 Alfred Street, Milsons Point, Sydney,
New South Wales 2061, Australia

Random House New Zealand Limited
18 Poland Road, Glenfield
Auckland 10, New Zealand

Random House (Pty) Limited
Isle of Houghton, Corner of Boundary Road & Carse O'Gowrie,
Houghton 2198, South Africa

Random House Group Limited Reg. No. 954009

www.randomhouse.co.uk

A CIP catalogue record for this book
is available from the British Library

Papers used by Random House are natural, recyclable
products made from wood grown in sustainable
forests. The manufacturing processes conform to
the environmental regulations of the country of origin.

ISBN 9780099498674 (from Jan 2007)
ISBN 0 09 949867 7

Printed and bound in Great Britain by
Cox & Wyman Ltd, Reading, Berkshire

For Dr. Greg Haines
and Missy Jones—
who reassembled the skeleton

The author wishes to acknowledge
forensics researcher/co-plotter
Matthew V. Clemens.
Further acknowledgments appear
at the conclusion of this novel.

"As those who study them have come to learn, bones make good witnesses—although they speak softly, they never lie and they never forget."

—Dr. Clyde Collins Snow,
forensics anthropologist

"The more *outré* and grotesque an incident is the more carefully it deserves to be examined, and the very point which appears to complicate a case is, when duly considered and scientifically handled, the one which is mostly likely to elucidate it."

—Sherlock Holmes,
The Hound of the Baskervilles,
by Arthur Conan Doyle

BONES™
BURIED DEEP

PROLOGUE

1944

ON A MOONLESS JUNE NIGHT, AL CAPONE'S
sleek teak motorboat skimmed like a child's tossed
stone across the surface of Lake Michigan.

The craft had been a gift from someone who owed
the crime boss a favor; Capone had climbed aboard
once, promptly gotten seasick, and vowed never to return.

But from time to time—even now, years after
Snorky's postprison retirement to Florida—the mob
boss's former business associates found use for the
craft. Not big enough to make runs to Canada for
whiskey back in Prohibition days, the craft would be
used by Capone's men to speed out onto the lake in
the middle of the night, to meet the bigger boats and
bring back small shipments.

Post-Prohibition, other kinds of contraband had
been smuggled by the speedboat, but tonight neither
booze nor narcotics were aboard—though passenger

Anthony Gianelli wished he had a flask or even a reefer about now, to ward off the chill.

No, tonight was a much different sort of run.

Behind the wheel, Johnny Battaglia squinted into the darkness. Wanting to avoid prying eyes, the pilot— a rather generous appellation, Gianelli thought—ran the boat without lights and had to struggle to see where they were going.

Neither the smartest nor most keen-eyed of the mob's loyal soldiers, Battaglia did have his strengths— tough as a nickel steak, brave as a bull, and loyal as an English bulldog, which he happened to closely resemble.

Like Gianelli, Battaglia was a made man, though they both knew that Gianelli was the brains of the operation—unlike his burly counterpart, Gianelli had management potential and was headed toward bigger and better things.

Taller, thinner, and more nattily attired than Battaglia, Gianelli was not an underboss yet, but he kept his eyes open and his mouth shut, and knew that tonight's assignment was the next rung on his personal ladder.

All they had to do was get through this run unscathed.

Gianelli did not want to be out here on the water, and he found vaguely unsettling the lights of Chicago fading into the darkness, barely a glimmer on the horizon; but this was his job, and he would do it.

Any trepidation he felt wasn't fear of being caught, not exactly—but his wife had just arrived home with their new son, Raymond, and he wanted to be with his family in case he was needed.

Granted, little remained for a father to do at this point—tending to the baby was, after all, woman's work. But he still felt like he should be home.

His job did allow a certain flexibility of hours, and thank God he wasn't overseas, in Europe steamrolling the Nazis, or worse, the Pacific fighting the Nips; like Sinatra, he had a punctured eardrum, thank you God.

Instead, here he was, bouncing along the water, part of a little navy in a different kind of war, wishing that he had brought his light overcoat. His suit jacket, an expensive gray pinstripe, was of little help against the wind cutting over the speedboat's windscreen.

Hell, it was June! But it was so damn cold out here on the water, in the middle of the night, might as well be March.

Battaglia had his shoulders hunched against the wind as well. In the back, on the deck, police captain Ed Hill showed no signs of the cold getting to him— of course, Hill had already been dead for four hours, and was pretty cold in a way that had nothing to do with the weather, a corpse wrapped inside a bedspread the size of one of those Caribbean banana republics.

This thought brought Gianelli a slight smile— gallows humor to a mob guy, as to any soldier, was the norm.

Hill was no ordinary copper. If he had been, anywhere here on the lake would have been good enough to drop him in.

But Hill had been a small but significant piece in the feds' case against Paul Ricca, the man who sat in the chair at the head of the Outfit table, from which Al Capone and then Frank Nitti had ruled Chicago. Ricca, "the Waiter," had been convicted last December and gone to Atlanta earlier this year for a ten-year stretch, leaving the capable if unimaginative Tony Accardo to run things in his absence.

Everybody knew Mr. Ricca was still in charge, but for now "Joe Batters"—a nickname given Accardo by Capone himself for the young thug's skill with a baseball bat (and not on a diamond)—was running the business.

Hill's role in getting Ricca sent away had earned him an official commendation . . . and Tony Accardo's wrath. Normally cops were off-limits; but this one had made the mistake of taking the Outfit's cash, and then ratting them out, anyway.

Tonight Gianelli and Battaglia had delivered a stern and terminal rebuke to Hill in his home. Mrs. Hill was out of town, visiting a sister in Milwaukee; had Gianelli not seen the woman board the train with his own eyes, he never would have whacked the cop in his own house.

Business was business, but they weren't savages.

No women, no children, that was the rule. Usually

no cops or reporters, unless they asked for it. If you didn't have rules, you were just as bad as the animals.

Gianelli peered down at the large lump in the bottom of the boat. He felt nothing—nothing—about this body on the deck: not anger, not hatred, not joy, not even indifference. Hill had crossed them and paid for it—this was the end result of a business transaction, nothing more.

No one associated with the Outfit wanted Hill to turn up, no bobbing to the surface or washing up on the beach for this bastard with a badge. Even *without* a body, there'd be heat. . . .

So they had other plans for Hill.

"That must be U.S. Steel," Battaglia yelled, working to be heard over wind and engine noise. He pointed at dim lights off to their right.

Starboard, Gianelli thought . . . or was it port? He was almost sure it was starboard.

"Yeah," Gianelli agreed, feeling like a schmuck for yelling back, when there were only the two of them . . . not counting the cop. Who sure as hell wasn't listening.

The lights seemed distant, pinpoints only slightly larger than the few stars that dotted the sky. "We're gettin' there," Gianelli said.

Battaglia nodded.

Another ten minutes and they would be well past the giant steel mill and approaching the barren sand dunes of the Indiana shore.

Accardo had sent word and a car would meet them. They would get rid of Hill for good, then back home by morning. That was the plan, anyway.

The U.S. Steel plant pumped out sheet metal three shifts a day—steel that would soon be tanks, flame throwers, ships, and God only knew what else in the war effort. Farther past the mill now, waves breaking on the beach were audible even over the engine thrum.

Battaglia angled the boat that way and cut the engine to a growl.

"See anything?" Battaglia asked.

Gianelli slowly scanned the shoreline—so dark was the night, he might have been staring down a gun barrel.

"Can't see a goddamn thing," he admitted.

Where was the car, and the son of a bitch who was supposed to meet them? Had there been some foul-up? Worse yet, a double cross?

Gianelli strained to make out a shape that might be a car in the darkness. But all he saw was the rise and fall of the dunes. There was the occasional house out here, but not in this stretch—that's why they'd picked it.

Only thing out here *should* be their contact . . .

"Where the hell is he?" Battaglia wondered.

Running parallel to the beach, motor idling, sand on their right, Gianelli could make out only the sound of the tide rolling up to slap the shore, the motion of the water moving them slowly forward and slightly right.

Starboard, Gianelli reminded himself.

Ahead of them, up the beach, he saw a glimmer of light . . .

. . . and then it was gone.

Had he seen it or imagined it?

"You catch that?" he asked.

"Catch what?" Battaglia replied, his face turned farther astern.

Maybe he *had* imagined it.

Gianelli looked again, harder, if that was possible, and waited. And waited some more. And some more . . .

There it was!

A small dot of light maybe fifty yards farther up the beach—a flashlight, no doubt about it.

"I see it," Battaglia said, and guided the boat in that direction.

As they neared the shore, Gianelli realized the guy was standing at the end of a short pier. Battaglia cut the engine so they could float in alongside the wooden structure, and the guy doused his light.

Battaglia tossed a line to the guy, who pulled them up to the dock and tied it off on a cleat.

As Battaglia and their host hefted the package out of the boat, Gianelli studied the beach, still unable to see the car in the moonless night.

"Where's your wheels?" he whispered, the nature of their activity calling for that tone more than any chance they'd be overheard.

"Closer to the road," the guy said.

Gianelli pulled a small flashlight from his jacket pocket and shone it in the man's face.

Man?

Hell, this guy was a kid, barely eighteen—curly black hair, wide brown eyes, and a face that looked like it never met a razor.

"Closer to the road?" Gianelli asked, keeping his voice down, knowing it carried at night.

"Yeah," the kid said matter-of-factly.

"Why the hell's it over there?" Battaglia asked, just a little irritated.

The kid let out a long breath as they rested the package on the dock.

"Either we carry this load closer to the road," he said, his baritone voice older than his face, "and toss it in the car, or I pull the car up here for us to stuff this guy in . . . and then explain to the cops why the car sank in the sand and we got stuck."

Battaglia still looked pissed, but Gianelli was nodding. "You got a brain or two, kid. What's your handle, anyway?"

"David Musetti," the kid said, his voice as hushed as Gianelli's.

"Good thinkin', Davey. Come on, Johnny, let's get this dead weight up to the car."

Fifteen minutes later, the body was stowed in the trunk of a '42 Chevy, while Battaglia was stuffed in the backseat, Gianelli sitting on the passenger side next to Musetti as the young man started the car.

"Know where you're goin'?" Battaglia asked.

"Yeah," Musetti said matter-of-factly—they might have been discussing what restaurant they were choosing. "Been there before."

They crossed the railroad tracks of the South Shore Line, a train that ran from the city to South Bend, Indiana. Gianelli and a couple of other mugs had even brought a body here in a trunk one time on the train.

The Dunes Express, the boys used to call it.

But lately it had been strictly delivery by car—the feds had infiltrated the railroad dicks, watching for wartime sabotage; so hauling corpses by rail was out.

The Musetti kid turned the Chevy right onto Highway 12 and switched on the car's headlights. They'd barely gone a mile when they passed an Indiana state trooper who had some poor bozo pulled over.

The cop was watching, smugly skeptical, as the drunk tried to walk a chalk line on the edge of the road.

Gianelli admired the fact that the kid neither sped up nor slowed down when he drove past the scene.

Gianelli said, "Kid, you're a pretty cool customer."

Musetti shrugged, then glanced into the mirror before turning left without a signal, easing onto a dirt road that was little more than a cow path.

The kid killed the lights.

They rode back into the woods almost half a mile, cresting a hill and easing down the other side before Musetti turned off the car.

They sat in silence for a moment before climbing out.

"Let's get to it," Battaglia said.

Funny how little emotion there was in it, Gianelli thought. He was a sucker for sad movies and had to work not to blubber at a funeral of a friend or family member (either family). And maybe even a bent flatfoot like Hill deserved better.

But that was how it was in war—bodies didn't get respect, just disposal, and the ones doing the disposing didn't feel anything much other than an itch to get done and get back home.

Gianelli grabbed the shovels while the other two lugged the body. The soil here was marshy and that would make the digging easy, but Gianelli wished he had thought to wear less expensive shoes.

The body was buried deep in no time. Gianelli wondered how Captain Ed Hill would feel if he knew how many of the *Mafiosi* he had chased over the years were interred around him.

"On Judgment Day," Gianelli said, "when all these corpses come up outa the ground, this poor bastard's gonna be way outnumbered."

Battaglia laughed.

Musetti didn't.

Soon the taciturn kid was pulling the car onto the

highway and retracing his route back to the dunes. As they ambled along, Gianelli reflected.

The marsh was home to many mysteries, Gianelli knew; and nobody would come out here looking for bodies. The sandy earth would keep its secrets forever.

Or till Judgment Day, anyway.

And maybe not even then. Gianelli laughed to himself, and Battaglia looked over at him stupidly.

What kind of angel would want to come out to these godforsaken boonies to resurrect anybody?

1

The Present

LIKE A THICK OIL SLICK SPREADING OVER LAKE Michigan, an oppressive wave of heat coated Chicago, as it had since early spring.

The summer-long drought, coupled since late July with a garbage strike, made for long nights and longer days in a city where aromas were high and tempers were short. Piles of garbage accrued over the last seven weeks had become giant disease-bearing compost heaps.

Op-ed writers for the newspapers were referring to Chicago as "Fecund City" and "The City of Big Smoulders," but neither side budged in the strike negotiations, and Mother Nature seemed to have decided to simply parboil the city.

In this town where smiles were rare about now,

Special Agent Seeley Booth sat in a meeting room of the Everett M. Dirksen Federal Building barely able to contain his grin.

He'd been working on the case against Chicago Mafia bosses Raymond and Vincent Gianelli for most of the last six months, and now—with the help of a Gianelli crony turned informant—Booth had father and son in his sights.

Sitting on the prosecution side of the table, Booth exuded quiet confidence. Which was, after all, part of the profile for an FBI agent; but with his square jaw, close-cropped brown hair, and steel-blue eyes, his confidence today approached cockiness.

Even though this wasn't a court day, Booth had worn his "testifying" suit, the number every law enforcement professional kept bagged in the closet for those special days in court.

Booth's was a charcoal gray with a lighter pinstripe and had cost him just a little less than his first car; but today he wanted to look as good as he felt.

Next to Booth, federal prosecutor Daniel Mc-Michael scribbled on a yellow legal pad that lay next to a stack of papers. His black hair receding and parted on the left, McMichael wore a gray suit easily twice as expensive as Booth's.

The prosecutor had dark eyes that could be warm and friendly to those on his side, and icy and aloof to his enemies. A bulbous nose squatted between high, chubby cheeks and over a mouth that turned up a couple of degrees at the corners in what passed for a smile.

Dan McMichael had the wide shoulders and strong arms of an athlete, compromised by the slightly soft look of one whose playing days were long behind him. If his career had been baseball instead of prosecution, McMichael would be the MVP who went on to become the crusty but benign manager who quietly passed advice to his high-strung young players.

Booth had worked a couple of cases with McMichael and respected the attorney's no-nonsense approach. They had carved out convictions both times and the perps were now spending long sentences in federal prisons.

To their left, sitting inconspicuously in a corner, was Anna Jones, a petite blonde court recorder with brown eyes and what Booth interpreted as a slightly openmouthed smile intended just for him.

Or perhaps that was just his confidence getting out of hand. . . .

Checking his watch, the FBI agent noted that—although he had expected the Gianellis to be here by now—they weren't officially late. The meeting had been scheduled for eleven and their prospective defendants still had a couple of minutes to make it on time.

And they did—at 10:59 and thirty seconds, the

door swung open and three men entered, single file.

First was Raymond Gianelli, brawny but elegant in a brown suit, chocolate-colored shirt, and brown-and-tan-striped tie. His eyes, a very light brown, followed this color coordination, but his hair was black and slicked back with a hint of gray at the temples; his tan tried too hard, Booth thought, the type that came from a tanning bed and not the beach.

Next came Raymond's son, Vincent.

Taller but thinner than his muscular father, his brown hair close-cropped, his eyes darker than Dad's, Vincent wore a brown herringbone suit a shade lighter than his father's. Handsome in a well-scrubbed fashion with a smile that was almost a sneer, he wore a light green shirt and solid tan tie. His brown Italian loafers no doubt cost more than Booth's expensive suit, and maybe McMichael's.

To the agent, Vincent Gianelli looked what he was: a textbook sociopath. The boy cared about no one but himself, with the possible exception of his father, a relationship that seemed built more on business than love for a family member, more Machiavellian than emotional.

The only other thing Vincent cared about was a huge Neapolitan mastiff named Luca, presumably named after Luca Brasi from *The Godfather*.

Booth knew this and more about his prey.

Mob guys could be oddly normal—basically decent people who through family ties and character defects went down a criminal path.

The Gianellis—Vincent in particular—were not in that group.

Trailing his clients, about the size of a Mini-Cooper, waddled Russell Selachi, the Gianelli family attorney.

The counselor wore a black suit, though its effect was not particularly slimming, with a white shirt with silver stripes, and a blue, pink, yellow, and green tie loud enough to have been snatched from a clown's clothesline.

Booth wondered if a dozen clowns would pile out, like they did out of those tiny cars in the circus, should Selachi open his coat. . . .

Even though the trio exuded arrogance, the Barnum and Bailey imagery brought a smile to Seeley Booth's face.

"Special Agent Booth," the elder Gianelli said in a resonant baritone, "you're in a surprisingly good mood for a man about to be sued for wrongful prosecution."

Booth allowed his smile to shift to a smirk. "I am in a good mood, thanks . . . and that would only be wrongful prosecution if you were innocent."

"Gentlemen," McMichael said, his voice stern as he shot a look at Booth.

The FBI agent returned the glance, his expression reassuring the prosecutor: *I'll behave, Dan.*

Turning his attention back to the others, McMichael said, "Have a seat, would you?"

The three men took chairs across the table, Raymond Gianelli in the center, Vincent on his left. Selachi withdrew a yellow pad from a briefcase, and set the pad before him and the briefcase beside him.

McMichael turned to the blonde recorder. "Ms. Jones?"

She gave him a curt nod.

"All right, then," McMichael said, looking across the table. "You ready, Mr. Selachi?"

"We are, Mr. McMichael."

"Well, then, let the record show who is in attendance today. Myself, Daniel McMichael, United States attorney; Special Agent Seeley Booth of the Federal Bureau of Investigation . . ."

Booth thought he caught Anna smiling at him again as she recorded his name. Wishful thinking?

". . . Raymond Gianelli," McMichael continued. "Vincent Gianelli . . ."

The younger Gianelli grinned at Anna, apparently thinking the smile had been for him—or was he mocking Booth?

The FBI agent tensed. Ms. Jones's smile vanished and she looked down at her flying fingers.

McMichael was saying, ". . . and Russell Selachi, attorney for the Gianellis. Both Raymond and Vincent Gianelli have been informed of their rights."

"So noted," Selachi said.

Shuffling some papers from the stack in front of him, McMichael said, "Let's get right to the heart of the matter . . . and begin with your command to have Marty Gramatica assassinated."

"Allegedly," Selachi said.

Vincent Gianelli's eyes burned. "That fucking liar Musetti. He's—"

"*Vincent,*" Selachi said.

Raymond Gianelli shot his son a look and Vincent eased back in his chair and folded his arms and found something interesting to look at on the paneled wall to his left.

Stewart Musetti was the reason they were all in this room today.

A childhood friend of Raymond's, son of Raymond's father's trusted lieutenant David Musetti, and a former Gianelli lieutenant himself, Stewart Musetti—thinking the family was about to hit him—had turned himself in and ratted out his former bosses in exchange for a future in the Federal Witness Protection Program.

Booth had, in recent months, come to know Musetti well.

Soft-spoken and almost devoid of personality, Musetti—a bald man with a gray wreath of hair and silver steel glasses—looked more like a math professor than a man allegedly responsible for at least twenty murders in thirty years of toiling for the Gianelli family.

When the longtime hitman had flipped, Booth had been there to catch him, and had spent the better part of a month interrogating Musetti, then another five weeks investigating his charges and collecting evidence that would corroborate his chief witness's story.

Now, thanks to Musetti's loose lips and Booth's hard work, the FBI agent had them.

The Gianellis were going down.

"The Gramatica murder," McMichael said, regaining control of the situation.

Raymond Gianelli shrugged. "A tragedy—an old friend, dearly missed. Did you have a question?"

"Yes. A simple one—did you order the murder?"

Selachi sat forward and half-smiled. "That isn't a serious question, surely. . . ."

Gianelli put a hand on his attorney's arm. "It's okay, Russell. It's okay. . . . Mr. McMichael, the answer is no, I did not order the murder of Marty Gramatica."

"You did not tell the man you ordered to do this to . . ." McMichael made a show of referring to his notes. ". . . 'Make sure the bastard doesn't wake up tomorrow'?"

Gianelli remained passive, though his eyes met McMichael's. He shrugged and opened his palms and smiled like an uncle addressing a beloved but slightly dim nephew.

"You have to understand," Gianelli said, "that I've known Stewart Musetti for a long time . . . practically all my life . . . but we had a falling-out over business matters, and Stewart feels, rightly or wrongly, that he was not treated fairly. That has made him bitter. We are adults here. We know that bitter men sometimes do things that are . . ."—Gianelli smiled at Booth— ". . . vengeful in nature. My son, in his understandable passion, spoke the truth: Musetti lies."

Leaning forward, McMichael asked, "Then Stewart Musetti is nothing more than a disgruntled employee with an ax to grind?"

"Bingo!" Vincent blurted, drawing another reproving glance from his father.

Booth was starting to understand something—he'd expected McMichael to depose the father and son separately, and had expressed his misgivings about dealing with them together half an hour before this meeting.

"It'll be fine," McMichael had said, bemused. "After all this time, Seeley, don't you trust me?"

"I trust you, Dan . . . but I think I've earned an explanation."

McMichael nodded. "Yes you have. . . . I'll ask both Papa and Junior questions now, some things we know they've done and we can get them for in any event. . . . Then, in a couple of days, I'll come up with some new questions, just for Vincent. Once we get him alone, and on the record, I'll go after the father—with hothead sonny boy's answers in my pocket."

"I guess that makes sense. . . ."

The prosecutor shrugged. "If nothing else, and these charges somehow get flushed like all the others, at least I might have a shot to get them for perjury."

McMichael had used the word "flushed" on purpose. Like the other federal prosecutors in the building, he was running scared.

As a young enforcer, Raymond Gianelli had been called "the Plumber" because he had a way of stopping leaks inside the mob. As Gianelli had climbed the ladder of command, the nickname stuck but changed in definition.

Each time new charges were brought, somehow "the Plumber" managed to get them "flushed." In a lifetime of working for, and later leading the largest mob family in Chicago, Gianelli had never spent a night in jail.

And right now Raymond Gianelli was staring at Prosecutor McMichael with dispassionate eyes.

"Despite what the people in this office think . . . and you FBI people, too, Agent Booth . . . we are simply in a family business here. Does it offend you, our Sicilian heritage? Is that why you seem determined to drag us down?"

This nonsense shattered Booth's ability to monitor

himself, and he heard himself say, "You're playing the *race* card? The 'man' is persecuting you? You gotta be kidding me. . . ."

"Mr. Booth," McMichael said.

Selachi raised his pen and pointed it at Booth. "You're overstepping, Agent Booth. You are badly over—"

Raymond Gianelli's voice, soft but powerful, cut his lawyer off. "Agent Booth," he said, "I resent your attitude and your implication. Marty Gramatica was my *friend,* for many, many years . . . *and* he was Vincent's friend. Why would I have him killed?"

Booth's control was back. "Because he crossed you."

Gianelli shrugged and waved that off. "So you say."

"I'm not the one who says," Booth said. "I'm just passing along what our witness tells us."

The mobster shrugged again, but was that a smile tickling the bastard's lips?

Booth felt a chill—he knew Uncle Sam had the Gianelli duo cold; so why was "the Plumber" smiling?

All of a sudden, Booth had the feeling that something was not right. . . .

As if picking up on Booth's mental cue, Special Agent Josh Woolfolk opened the door and made an awkward picture of himself, framed there.

"Mr. Woolfolk, we are very busy," McMichael said, annoyed.

"Yes, sir, I know, and I'm sorry, but . . ."

Woolfolk completed his sentence with a gesture, curling a finger toward Booth, summoning him to the hall.

McMichael's eyes darted back and forth between the two FBI men.

And everyone on the Gianelli side of the table sat back and relaxed.

When they were alone in the hallway, Woolfolk glanced both ways. Shorter than Booth, thinner, but older, Woolfolk had dark hair swept to the right and dark, puffy eyes that gave him an exhausted look.

"What?" Booth asked, growing more peevish by the second.

"It's . . . it's . . . Moose . . ."

"Moose?" Booth asked, frowning in confusion.

"Musetti," Woolfolk finally managed.

Everything inside Booth stilled, much as it had in his military days, when he was a sniper and had acquired the target.

Everything around him slowed, everything within seemed to stop. He breathed without breathing, felt no nerves, no tension, no anything.

There was only him, the trigger, and the target.

Right now the target was Woolfolk. "What *about* Musetti?"

"He is *gone*."

The inner stillness exploded. "Where?"

Woolfolk, eyes hysterical, said, "No damn idea."

Booth took a deep breath, refocused on the target. "What about the four agents guarding him?"

The other agent swallowed and shrugged. "Gone, too."

"Gone, too?" Booth echoed. "Where . . . how . . . ?"

"No clue."

Booth's mind raced. "When was the last time we had contact with them?"

"They checked in from the safe house this morning right before breakfast," Woolfolk said. "A pair of agents showed up with lunch and found the place empty . . . like it had been abandoned."

Hands on his hips, Booth loomed over his fellow agent. "And we haven't heard from any of them since?"

"Not a word."

Prosecutor McMichael came out into the hall, carefully shutting the door behind him. "What's going on?" he hissed.

Booth and Woolfolk exchanged a look.

Booth said, "They've all disappeared."

The prosecutor's face turned to stone. "Who? What . . . ?"

Booth explained what he had just learned.

"Musetti and four FBI agents?" McMichael asked, his voice cracking. "*Vanished?* How the hell is that possible?"

"I wouldn't know," Booth said, eyes on the closed door. "And the people who *do* know aren't likely to tell us. . . . No wonder that bunch was so smug this morning—they knew damn well Musetti was about to disappear, and what better alibi for them than being deposed by a federal prosecutor and the FBI agent who had been hounding their asses?"

McMichael's eyes were on that closed door, as well.

"We're going to lose them," the prosecutor whispered. Despair edged his words. "The Plumber's going to get another set of charges flushed."

"Right now," Booth said, "I'm more interested in the lives of four FBI agents."

"Of course you are," McMichael said, chagrined. "Of course you are."

Woolfolk said, "I've got the Chicago PD crime scene unit on the way to the safe house. . . ."

"Good."

". . . and we've got agents working every angle we can think of."

Nodding to Woolfolk, Booth opened the door and walked back in. He was only vaguely aware that the other two men followed.

He circled the table and looked down, his eyes boring into Raymond Gianelli's.

The Mafioso didn't flinch.

Booth's immediate urge was to slam Gianelli into the wall, screw his pistol in the man's ear, and question him about the whereabouts of the four missing agents . . .

. . . but that would cost more than it would gain.

He continued to stare at Gianelli, willing the emotion away, calming the anger, becoming the sniper again.

His voice steady, he asked, "You want to tell me where they are?"

Gianelli squinted. "*Who* are *where* . . . ?"

"You want to make a deal," Booth said, "now's the time." He thumped the wooden surface between them. "This is the *only* time there will ever be anything on the table for you *or* your son."

Shrugging with a single shoulder, Gianelli said, "You don't seem to understand, Agent Booth—innocent parties don't need deals. And I'm an innocent party. It's the guilty parties who need to make deals, and I'm not one of them."

Booth said nothing, temper in check. He wouldn't waste time here with this scum when fellow agents were in harm's way.

He said, "All right, that's enough for today."

"You want us to leave?" Vincent Gianelli asked. "After we came all the way down here?"

McMichael chimed in his approval of Booth's call, saying, "Yes—other related matters have taken precedence."

Booth said, "As you well know."

The elder Gianelli rose, smiling. "I'll tell you what I 'know,' Agent Booth—I know harassment when I see it. I know when a guy is spinning his wheels and wasting my time."

Booth said nothing.

Attorney Selachi was shaking his head. "We made a great effort here at a considerable inconvenience to my clients and—"

McMichael cut him off. "We have an emergency. There will be no deposition today."

When the others had cleared out, Booth followed Woolfolk down through the building to the parking lot.

The two agents immediately headed to the safe house where Musetti had been held in a small Indiana community just the other side of Gary.

The thinking had been that if they moved Musetti out of the Chicago metro area, their witness could be guarded more effectively. Booth's superiors had picked a small gated community called Ogden Dunes inside the Indiana Dunes National Lakeshore Park.

Booth had considered it an excellent location for a safe house; but, obviously, it had not been safe enough. . . .

Even with the red lights flashing, Woolfolk spent an hour getting through midday Chicago traffic, driving around Gary, then finally turning left onto the long two-lane blacktop that led to the tiny burg of Ogden Dunes.

The first thing a visitor saw upon approaching this semi-private community on the south shore of Lake Michigan was a speed bump the size of a Native American burial mound; the second thing was a guard shack with a huge stop sign hanging from a metal pole just outside.

Normally, a uniformed guard would come out, ask the entering motorist his or her destination, then phone ahead.

For the last ten days, that guard had been one of four FBI agents assigned to Stewart Musetti. In his turn, each went undercover in the security company uniform.

Now, as Woolfolk eased the Crown Victoria up to the guard shack, the pretense was gone.

Two men approached the stopped car, each wearing the typical gray suit and dark glasses of special agents.

The one from the shack on the passenger side came up to Booth's window, pistol drawn, his arm hanging down so the pistol was almost hidden behind his leg.

The agent on the driver's side approached holding an MP5 at port arms and leaned down to address Woolfolk, who already had his ID out.

To Booth, all this was the Bureau equivalent of closing the barn door long after the horse was gone. Hell, the horse, four riders, the saddle, their case, his career. . . .

Booth powered down his window to show his ID to the tall blond agent who took off his dark glasses to reveal light blue eyes as he studied the ID nearly identical to his own. Booth had seen the man in the Chicago office but had no idea what his name was.

The agent gave Booth a polite nod and put his glasses back on.

"What the hell happened?" Booth asked him.

The agent looked at him, said nothing, then offered up an almost imperceptible shrug.

On the other side of the car, the other guard waved Woolfolk through.

Woolfolk followed the blacktop another quarter mile, turned right onto a side street, and parked in front of the third house on the right.

Two police cars were parked on the street along with two more Crown Vics and a Chicago PD evidence tech van angled into the driveway of a sprawling white two-story clapboard house with black shutters on half a dozen windows.

Getting out, Booth noticed that other than the police cars, which had brought out a few gawkers, the neighborhood looked much as it had the day he had scouted the house—just like every other block in this tiny town hunkered next to the lake . . . quiet, unassuming, anonymous.

The Gianellis had a long reach, but the only way they could have found this place was from someone inside the Bureau—a prospect that added nausea to the rage boiling in Booth's belly.

Seeley Booth had two priorities now—find Stewart Musetti; and find the sellout in the Bureau who had leaked the location of the safe house.

"Who's in charge?" Booth asked as Woolfolk caught up with him on the sidewalk.

Both men were sticking their IDs in their breast pockets to identify themselves.

"Dillon," Woolfolk said. "He's probably inside."

Robert Dillon—always Robert, never Bob, which led to bad jokes about the singer—was Special Agent in Charge of the Chicago office; a hard-ass, but always fair. Booth respected him.

Booth and Woolfolk walked up to the front door. As they approached, two Chicago evidence techs exited carrying their cases.

One was a tall African-American guy—BELL, according to his name tag. The other was a red-haired woman nearly as tall and thin as her partner; her name tag read: SMITH.

"Anything?" Booth asked.

The woman gave them a glum smile. "Not much."

Bell shook his head. "Place is cleaner than my apartment."

The evidence techs continued on to their van while Booth and Dillon opened the front door.

The living room was empty but for the rent-to-own-style furnishings. A couch sat against one wall, two chairs at angles next to it, a television perched on a stand underneath a huge window.

Booth put his hand against the TV screen—cool.

The two agents passed through into a dining room. Four chairs surrounded a rectangular oak table, place mats on the table, sun streaming through thin curtains from three windows. The room seemed as if it was just waiting for someone to set out lunch.

In the kitchen, they found an agent Booth knew from the academy, a wide-shouldered, ruddy-faced guy named Mike Stanton.

Counters running down the two sides, refrigerator on the right, stove and microwave on the left, the spacious kitchen had an island in the middle and a breakfast nook in the back right corner.

The breakfast dishes were still on the table, the attack probably coming mid-meal. Nothing seemed amiss, meaning the agents hadn't even had the chance to draw their weapons.

"Booth," Stanton said by way of greeting.

"Hey. Where's Dillon?"

"Out back with the locals. Trying to figure out if they could have gone out that way."

Through the back door, Booth went down the few stairs into the yard, Woolfolk on his heels.

Dillon was out there, all right—a square-shouldered, square-jawed man of fifty, his dark hair swept straight back, his dark eyes cold as they scanned the area. His sharp nose gave him the appearance of an eagle.

Two uniformed officers and two local detectives fanned out around Dillon, wearing that horrible frustrating expression that meant they not only were unable to find what they were searching for, they didn't *know* what they were searching for.

Booth approached the group and Dillon raised his chin in greeting.

"What went down here?" Booth asked.

Dillon shrugged. "They came in through the main gate, grabbed the guard, then your guess is as good as mine. . . . The bad guys probably used the agent playing guard as a hostage, to bargain for Musetti. But we don't even know that for sure."

"Jesus," Booth muttered.

"All we know for sure is Musetti and our boys are simply not here . . . and no sign of a struggle. No neighbors saw or heard anything. Even the car is gone. The detectives are going to canvass the neighbors down toward the lake, to see if they could have gotten out that way. May be our intruders had a boat waiting."

"In broad daylight, on a hot summer day with people on the beach?" Booth asked. "Doubtful."

"Agreed," Dillon said. "But no stone gets left

unturned on this one. I want you in charge, Seeley."

"We're in agreement already. But what about the Gianelli case?"

Dillon's features hardened. "Without Musetti, there is no Gianelli case."

"No argument there, either."

"Good. Make it happen, Booth—find Musetti. Find our four agents."

"Yes, sir."

Dillon gestured. "Woolfolk will work with you. Find Musetti and save our collective ass."

Booth knew a dismissal when he heard it. He turned, but before he could take a step, Dillon's voice halted him.

"We'll get what little we have on your desk by the end of the day. In the meantime, start beating the bushes. . . . See if anybody on the street knows anything."

"Yes, sir."

At midnight, Booth was still at his desk, everyone else having cleared out, when a call from the night guard brought him to the lobby, where he found four FBI agents waiting . . .

. . . the four FBI agents who had been babysitting Musetti.

One still wore the security uniform from the guard shack.

He said when he went up to a car, men with automatic weapons came out of the woods and took him prisoner. Then, as Dillon had suspected, the attackers had gone to the house and used him to get inside and snatch Musetti.

"They had us blindfolded," the agent told Booth. "Wrists and ankles duct-taped—took us in a truck of some kind, and drove us around in circles till we were so goddamn disoriented, I don't think any of us has any idea where we were. . . ."

Booth took them upstairs and questioned them at length, but little else was learned.

None of the agents could tell Booth where they had been, and Musetti had been transported in a separate vehicle . . . and they all assumed their witness was already dead.

No argument there, either.

However hopeless it might look, for the next forty-two days, Seeley Booth sought Stewart Musetti like the hitman was the holy grail.

The FBI agent worked sixty- to eighty-hour weeks, stopping only to eat and sleep.

He interviewed Musetti's girlfriend, his ex-wife, the Gianellis, every man, woman, or child with even the most tenuous connection to the Gianelli family . . . and learned nothing.

What meager evidence had been collected from the safe house was tested and chased down, and each piece led to its own dead end.

Six weeks and all he had to show for his search was a pile of files leading nowhere, bags under his eyes, and the feeling that Stewart Musetti was gone for good . . . and he strongly suspected the same was true of the government's case against Raymond and Vincent Gianelli.

Hot summer gave way to a warm autumn.

The garbage strike finally got settled. The drought continued, but the humidity was down, which at least gave Chicago a more tolerable climate.

One thing had not changed since that first awful day: Booth working until midnight.

On night forty-three, he was about to pack it in when the phone rang and he picked it up. "Booth."

"Special Agent Booth, this is Barney."

". . . Barney?"

"You know—guard in the lobby?"

"Oh yeah. Sorry, Barney, didn't recognize your voice."

"You're about the only one left in the building, sir. So I thought I better start with you. I've got something down here somebody needs to see. Probably you."

Booth was in no mood for practical jokes, whether Barney's or some vandal's. "What is it?"

The guard took a long moment before answering. "It's . . . well, it's bones, sir. I guess you'd say—it's a, you know . . . skeleton?"

Hanging up the phone, Booth threw on his jacket and hustled to the elevator.

Two minutes later he was in the lobby, where he found gray-haired, pot-bellied Barney staring out through the glass panes that made up the lobby.

Just outside, on the sidewalk of Plymouth Square, Booth saw something too. He exited the building, Barney on his tail, and looked down at a fully articulated human skeleton.

He scanned the area, thinking this might indeed be some elaborate pre-Halloween practical joke . . . but he saw no one.

Booth had a sinking feeling that this was all that was left of his star witness.

Under the mercury vapor lights illuminating Plymouth Square, the bones appeared very white, almost bleached. Squatting next to the skeleton, Booth saw something that struck him as odd, even in this already strange situation.

Tiny wires holding the bones together.

Someone had taken time to assemble the skeleton like one of those seen hanging in the science room back in Booth's junior high days.

Between the bones of the foot, not quite a toe tag, Booth saw a folded piece of paper.

A note?

His curiosity told him to pick it up; his training told him not to.

He glanced one more time toward the toe-held note, then pulled his cell phone from his jacket.

"What do you want me to do?" Barney asked from behind him.

"Call 911 and tell 'em what we've got. I'll watch the body until you get back."

"Yeah, I, uh . . . guess he ain't goin' anywhere."

"I guess not, Barney. But you are."

The guard nodded and hustled off.

Booth punched in Woolfolk's number, and when the sleepy agent picked up the phone, Booth outlined the situation.

"Is it Musetti?" Woolfolk asked.

"It's just a frickin' skeleton," Booth growled. "How the hell would I know?"

"Okay, okay. . . . What do you want me to do?"

"Get your ass down here. I want to see the security video from this building, the surrounding buildings, and any traffic light cameras in a six-block radius. Somebody left us a hell of a present, and I want to know where to send the thank-you card."

They clicked off and Booth went back to staring at the pile of bones in front of him.

Musetti?

Maybe. But like he had told Woolfolk, how the hell would he know?

The good news was, he knew someone who *would* know, someone who could tell him exactly whose skeleton had been dumped in Plymouth Square tonight.

He checked his watch—east coast was an hour later, nearly two a.m. out there.

She was going to be pissed, but Booth couldn't afford to care right now—he needed help. Her kind of help.

He punched in the number and hit the green button.

2

TEMPERANCE BRENNAN WAS ANNOYED.

And with Special Agent Seeley Booth at the root of her annoyance, this could hardly be described as a new feeling.

Back on her table at the Jeffersonian Institute, an eight-hundred-year-old Native American, with an arrowhead imbedded in his body, awaited her attention. And that was where she, and her attention, would prefer to be . . . and where she had been, in fact, burning the midnight oil until Dr. Goodman had called and told her that Booth had requested her services.

She had barely had time to rush home, pack a bag, and get to the airport before the plane took off. She would rather be back in the lab with her new eight-hundred-year-old friend right now, who would be demanding in his way, certainly . . . but not nearly so much as the FBI's Seeley Booth.

Instead, here she stood, gripping her forceps, its jaws open, inches above a generic Chicago hotel room bedspread.

When had the call come? Two a.m. or so—then the early morning flight, and now, not even noon local time, and she was checked into a downtown hotel . . . not having slept in over twenty-four hours.

So not surprisingly, her hand trembled with exhaustion as she closed the jaws of the forceps around the material of the bedspread.

Not even in the room ten minutes, she couldn't wait to get the spread off. She lifted and pulled, the bedspread coming with her, and without touching it with her free hand, she deposited the loathsome thing onto the floor in a corner of the room.

Her behavior might have seemed eccentric for a scientist like herself; but in reality, she was thinking exactly like a scientist, albeit a slightly paranoid one.

An all-too-credible urban myth among cops and forensic scientists was that the DNA expert who tested the Indianapolis hotel bedspread in the Mike Tyson rape trial had found over one hundred DNA deposits, none of them Tyson's, on the spread from that seven-hundred-fifty-dollar-a-night hotel room.

Brennan was not the only expert in the forensic field to avoid hotel bedspreads ever since.

Resting the forceps on the nightstand, Brennan flopped, fully clothed, onto the blanket, her head pressing into the kiss of the soft pillow. She tried to relax and shut off her brain—no small feat, especially today.

She heard something in the distance, some sort of tapping, but she could not put her finger on exactly what it was.

After a brief lull, she heard it again.

The third time she heard the sound, she realized someone was knocking at the door. She had fallen asleep after all; but whether for ten seconds or ten hours, she had no clue.

She flicked a glance at the red LED numbers of the clock: 5:17 p.m. Over four hours had disappeared.

Again, someone knocked on the door and she managed to rise, cringe at her hair in the dresser mirror, then wobble to the door and look through the peephole.

As if she needed to have bothered.

Opening the door, she glared at Special Agent Seeley Booth. His face was serious, possibly with worry; then when he focused on her, he gave her a lopsided grin.

"Hey, Bones," he said. "Thanks for coming."

"Haven't I asked you to stop calling me that?"

"Well . . . that's the first time today."

This exchange did not quell her urge to deliver her visitor a full frontal kick.

Booth brushed past her into the room.

"So you're just barging into my room now?"

"I didn't barge," Booth said, turning back to her. "Anyway, you were about to invite me, weren't you, Bones?"

"I still haven't decided. And will you *please* stop calling me that—you know I hate it."

"Most females would consider that a compliment."

"*Would* they?"

He wheeled and patted the air with his palms, put on the lopsided grin again, though his voice was serious.

"Look," he said, "this is an emergency, Bo . . . Dr. Brennan. I really need help. I've been knocking on your door every hour on the hour—got to where I thought maybe you'd lapsed into a coma."

She suddenly realized the "short lulls" between knocks had been a lot longer than she had perceived them.

"It's called sleeping, Booth. You called me in the middle of the night. I needed rest. Don't *you* sleep?"

"That's what the plane ride was supposed to be for. . . . Listen, I'm sorry I didn't call you directly about this, but you know all about channels. And I wouldn't pull you out of bed if it wasn't for something important . . ."

They both knew that had sounded a little wrong, and she glanced away while Booth skipped a beat, then went on.

"Look, you haven't had to put up with me for several months, because . . ."

"I don't need a reason for that. I'm perfectly content to go with the flow, on that one."

". . . I'm on an important case, maybe the biggest mob investigation since Gotti. We have a key witness missing, and now somebody dumped a skeleton on our doorstep last night—literally. I need to know all you can tell me about these particular bones."

"A human skeleton?" she asked.

"No," he said in sarcastic frustration, "it's a frog."

They both knew it was supposed to be a joke and they finally exchanged smiles—granted, small, nervous ones—after which they stood in silence while Booth searched for words.

She knew the feeling—Angela Montenegro, her best friend at the Jeffersonian, would have the perfect comeback here, but Brennan could not think of *anything* to say.

When in doubt, stick to business.

Brennan asked, "Where is this skeleton?"

"The Everett M. Dirksen Federal Building."

Brennan arched an eyebrow. "You weren't kidding about your doorstep. That's downtown, right?"

"Right. Where the FBI office is."

"It's almost as if somebody's *trying* to make this a federal matter."

He grunted something that was almost a laugh. "Isn't it, though? Somebody's thumbing their nose at us."

"Then I better take a look at the . . . well, it's *kind* of a crime scene, isn't it?"

"Yeah," Booth said dryly. "For littering . . ."

"Then the first thing we'll do is our bit to keep Chicago's sidewalks beautiful—and move that skeleton."

She grabbed her bag.

Booth was giving her that thoughtful wince of his, the one he got when he was a step behind her mentally; he got it a lot, she'd noticed.

"*Move* it?" he asked.

She led him out of the room and down the hall toward the elevator, saying, "Unless you FBI boys and girls have got a worktable handy in that federal building, with all the right tools, computer enhancements, and—"

"I get it," Booth interrupted. "You want your lab."

"Well," she said, turning to him with her best withering smile, "seems to me it would've been cheaper, and more efficient, to fly the *skeleton* to me, than to fly me to *it* . . . which, if you'd bothered to talk to me personally last night, I could have told you."

Booth punched the DOWN button with a little more force than he probably needed to. "Look, sue me—I wanted you here."

"And here I am."

"Bones, the case is here—the answers are here."

"But the *lab* is in Washington."

He turned to her and his expression was conciliatory. "We'll find you something suitable in Chicago."

The elevator doors opened. They had the car to themselves, but that didn't encourage conversation, and they stared at the floor indicator like strangers awkwardly avoiding each other.

She considered her dilemma.

If Booth had done the sensible thing and arranged the transfer of the skeleton, she could be doing the work in her own lab back home, with all the support and bells and whistles and her own bed at night, too. With her own bedspread.

But that was spilt milk under the bridge, right?

"Field Museum," she said.

"What? How—would *they* have a lab? Aren't they the dinosaur place?"

She smiled. "Spoken like a true eight-year-old."

He shrugged. "Look—I'm not exactly the museum type."

"I noticed."

Ignoring her dig, he said, "Over by the lake, right?"

"Yeah. Not the aquarium and not the Museum of Science and Industry. The Jeffersonian has a good relationship with the Field. If you like, I can call Dr. Goodman and—"

"No. Leave it to me. You need to see the bones where they were dumped, or should I have 'em moved to the museum?"

"You have photographs of the crime scene?"

"Does a dog have fleas?"

"Then go ahead and move the skeleton. Save us time."

They got out at the first floor and Booth had his cell phone in hand.

By the time the valet brought his Crown Vic, he had pulled strings to get her a workroom at the Field Museum. Bureau agents would transport the skeleton to the museum and it would be there not long after they arrived, if not sooner.

As they sped down Lake Shore Drive, Booth behind the wheel, Brennan hanging on for dear life as he dodged traffic, she couldn't help but wonder if this was how she was spending her last moments on the planet.

"Are you trying to get us killed?" she asked when he missed a delivery truck by less than a foot.

"I'm in a hurry," he said. He shook his head. "Would you please make up your mind?"

"About what?"

Booth flashed a glare, but it wasn't wholly unfriendly. "Are you timid, or foolhardy? I can never quite peg that."

"That's because I'm a riddle wrapped in an enigma."

"Oh. Good to know. . . . But I'm in a hurry 'cause I also want to know something else—specifically, what's in that goddamned note."

"Uh . . . what 'goddamned' note would that be?" she asked.

"The note on his—or her—foot."

She frowned. "A toe tag, you mean?"

Booth shook his head. "Something else."

"You didn't read it?"

"I wanted to keep it all together until you got here. I know what a stickler you are about stuff like that."

" 'Stuff' like evidence?"

"Look, Bones, I am not a moron. I just know you want the whole picture. And I know enough to preserve the evidence at any crime scene . . . littering or not. Cut me a break."

She blew out a sigh. "I didn't mean to snap at you . . . Just tired. . . . But why didn't you just carefully remove the note and read it?"

"Because this was . . . you know . . . *bones.* And you always get after me when I touch something. Now you're going after me because I *didn't*

touch something? How do I win with you, anyway?"

Brennan wondered why she and Booth could not
get through five minutes without sparring. Angela
claimed, in her *Cosmo* psychology 101 shorthand, that
it was "sexual tension."

Brennan had another theory.

She knew damn well she spent too much time with
dead people—who after all didn't talk back—and her
social skills were rusty. Still, that didn't mean she
needed to work at having an extended relationship
with every man who crossed her path, which sometimes seemed Angela's aim for her.

"Sorry," she muttered to Booth.

The dead were less complicated, easier to commu-
nicate with, and at the end of the day, she might actually help one of them find their way home, back to
their family.

How many live people could she say that
about?

Certainly not Pete, her ex. If anything, she had only
managed to help him become more lost in life's tangle.
But blaming herself about that was dumb—truth was,
Pete had a pretty good head start at losing his way before he met Brennan.

All she knew was, at this moment on her personal
path, Temperance Brennan was a lot more comfortable with the skeletal remains she'd be meeting at the

Field than with ninety-nine percent of the living men around her. She glanced at Booth—present company excepted.

Sometimes.

Booth spent the rest of the drive explaining to Brennan about his missing witness, Stewart Musetti, and his concerns about the ID of the skeleton that would greet them at the Field.

They were met at the entrance of the museum by an attractive Asian-American woman about as tall and slender as Brennan. The woman wore a white lab coat over a red V-neck blouse and black slacks, her raven hair hanging to her shoulders. She had wide-set dark eyes, a straight nose, and small, perfect white teeth that gleamed when she smiled, which she did as she extended her hand.

"Special Agent Booth, I'm Dr. Jane Wu."

He shook her hand and gave her that big puppy dog grin of his. Predictable.

"Very nice to meet you," Booth said. Then, nodding toward Brennan, he said, "This is—"

"Dr. Temperance Brennan," Dr. Wu said, shaking Brennan's hand, too. "Your reputation precedes you. I can't tell you what a pleasure it is to finally meet you."

"Nice to meet you, too," Brennan said.

"You've heard of her?" Booth asked the Field scientist.

Dr. Wu nodded. "Dr. Brennan and her staff at the Jeffersonian are respected worldwide for the work they do."

Booth summoned half a grin. "Well, I know Bones here is one of the best, but I didn't know her rep was so—"

Dr. Wu interrupted Booth again, staring wide-eyed at Brennan. "He calls you 'Bones'?"

Brennan smirked at the FBI agent. "Yes, and I've repeatedly asked him not to."

Dr. Wu gave the FBI man a disappointed look, and said, "How can you be so disrespectful, Special Agent Booth?"

He found the rest of that grin and shrugged. "Well, we're friends . . . sort of . . . certainly colleagues, and—"

Holding up a hand to silence him, Dr. Wu said, "Special Agent Booth—if they made baseball cards for anthropology, Dr. Brennan's would be a Ken Griffey Jr. rookie card."

Shaking her head and wincing at their host, Brennan said, "I have no idea what you just said."

Dr. Wu grinned. "That's all right. I understand that you have no need to speak 'guy' . . . but I am conversant in their native tongue. Have to be, around this town—let's just say I've explained your value in terms a man can understand."

"Yeah, and I get it," Booth said cheerfully.

Brennan, who found Dr. Wu's attitude a little patronizing toward her partner, said, "That wasn't exactly a compliment, Booth."

"Sure it was. She compared you to—"

"No, I meant compliment to *you*."

He shrugged. "Doesn't bother me. I get what she was saying."

Dr. Wu's cell phone rang and she fished it out of the pocket of her lab coat. "Yes?"

She listened for a moment, said, "Thanks," and ended the call.

"Sorry," she said to them. "But that was my boss telling me your package just came in through the back door. Would you like to see it?"

"Yes," Brennan said.

Skirting the information desk, the box office, and the short lines of people waiting to get in, Brennan and Booth followed Dr. Wu to the right, where she unlocked a door and hustled them through.

They were now in a long, stark, white-walled corridor with maybe three or four doors on the right-hand side.

Dr. Wu unlocked the first door and held it open while they entered—this time, into a gray concrete stairwell.

They stopped on the landing and waited for their

host to lock the door, then Dr. Wu led them down. Their footfalls echoed like gunshots against the concrete.

Brennan asked, "How long have you been here, Dr. Wu?"

"Started as an intern while I went to school—first at Northwestern, for my B.S.; then Loyola for my master's and Ph.D."

"Ah," Brennan said.

"So, to answer your question, about fifteen years. Started out sweeping floors and worked my way up. I was even a docent for a while . . . but mostly I've been behind the scenes down here."

At the bottom of the stairs, Dr. Wu unlocked another door, then led them down a dim hallway to a door on the left, this one unlocked.

They entered a large, antiseptic-smelling chamber lined floor to ceiling with wood drawers on three walls. Three large, rectangular worktables took up most of the center space and the door wall held shelving units filled with tools and chemicals.

Though not as modern or well lighted as her own work space, to Brennan this felt like home.

It was home, too, to a black body bag that lay on the center table.

"Your John Doe skeleton," Dr. Wu said.

Before they did anything else, both anthropologists donned lab coats and latex gloves. Then Brennan stepped forward, Dr. Wu moving around to the far side of the table to be of assistance if needed.

Carefully, Brennan unzipped the bag.

She noticed two things immediately.

One, the skeleton was wired together; and two, several of the bones were discolored.

Also, the bones bore a faint odor of earth. Brennan was not one to jump to conclusions, but she thought this skeleton might have spent some time buried.

"Could just be a hoax," she said to Booth.

"A hoax?" he asked, his voice a little nervous as he looked from Dr. Wu to Brennan.

"When was the last time you found a wired skeleton in the field?"

He thought about that, and his expression told Brennan he didn't like what he was thinking. "Never."

"So the odds of this being your witness . . ."

"Okay, I've got to admit that I might have been a little overeager in my assessment."

She frowned at him. "No one else at the scene thought it might have come from a school science room or something?"

Offering a sheepish smile, he said, "I'm with the FBI, Bones—people don't question what we say all that much."

"Maybe they should."

"Look, I did notice that wire myself, and it reminded me of a classroom display . . . but that wasn't my call."

No, Brennan thought, your *call was to my boss*. . . .

"Booth, do you know how easy it would be for someone to get their hands on one of these things and dump it in your lap?"

"I suppose it's possible," Booth said.

Both women were smiling now, and the agent frowned defensively.

"What?" Booth asked.

Dr. Wu said, "She's just messing with you. Although it *is* legal to buy human bones in the United States, a real skeleton would cost well over a thousand dollars . . . while a plastic one would do the same job for around three hundred."

"Still," Brennan said, "there are some real skeletons still in use at academic facilities—less common than it used to be; and usually they are small skeletons, coming from India. . . . But that doesn't mean we don't have a prank here."

Booth's eyes tightened. "No?"

"No. A nasty, ugly one—bones from a graveyard?"

"Oh."

"But I doubt that . . ."

"Why?"

"I smell earth on these bones."

He cocked his head. "Well, wouldn't that tend to indicate a graveyard . . . ?"

She shook her head. "Not really. Most bodies are

interred in caskets; burying a body directly into the ground is hardly usual."

"Yeah. Of course. You're right."

Brennan and Dr. Wu removed the skeleton from the body bag.

With the container out of the way and the remains laid out on the table, Brennan did a cursory exam. She looked at Dr. Wu. The other woman had seen the same things Brennan had—it was in her eyes.

"Booth," Brennan said. "This is not a hoax. Or anyway, if it's a prank, it's a very expensive one."

"You're sure?"

"For one thing, these bones are not plastic—I can tell you that. They are very much the real thing."

"You can tell already? Is it Musetti? . . . Sorry. I know that's impossible. . . ."

She raised an eyebrow. "Actually not impossible."

"Yeah?"

"Usually, I would need some sort of reference material from the victim to positively ID him . . . but in this case I can tell you this skeleton is definitely *not* Stewart Musetti. Or, more accurately, I can tell you it's not *all* Stewart Musetti."

"Obviously," Booth said. "Last time I saw the guy, he had a lot more skin and hair and, uh, meat on his bones."

Brennan shook her head. "You don't understand."

"I don't?"

"This skeleton is not made up of the body of just one person."

Booth's eyes widened. "Say what . . . ?"

"This is a contrived skeleton," Brennan said.

"What the hell—"

Dr. Wu tried to help. "One obvious place is the femora. You know what those are, right?"

"The big bones in the thigh."

"That's right, Agent Booth," Dr. Wu said. "And look at these two. Do you notice any differences?"

Stepping forward, Booth studied the right femur, which, judging from his expression, appeared pretty normal to him, though he obviously wasn't sure what he was supposed to be searching for.

Brennan watched her colleague with great interest.

He leaned over farther and examined the left femur. He pointed to dark lines that ran around the knobs on either end.

"This one's been broken?" he asked, his answer more of a question.

Dr. Wu gave him a tiny smile. "You found the right clue—but you drew the wrong conclusion."

Booth's eyes rolled. "It *wasn't* broken?"

Moving to one of the drawers in the wall, Dr. Wu pulled it open and extracted two long bones. She held up one that looked nearly identical to the left femur of the skeleton. This one had the same thin, dark lines.

"When we're born," Dr. Wu said, "our bones are not fully formed. The shaft is bone, but the epiphysial cap . . ."

Booth gave her a look.

". . . the *knobby* part has cartilage on the end that slowly turns to bone. The line shows us that the cartilage has not completely fused."

Booth nodded, getting it. "The left femur belonged to someone younger than the body the right femur came from."

"Good," Brennan said, meaning it.

"So," Booth said, frowning in thought, "how old *are* they?"

"The right femur," Brennan said, picking up the other bone Dr. Wu had gotten out of the drawer, "is fully fused. This bone came from an adult."

"The left one?"

Dr. Wu said, "A teenager. Someone younger than twenty."

Nodding, Booth asked, "Anything else readily apparent to the expert eye?"

"The pelvis belongs to a man," Brennan said. "The subpubic angle is more v-shaped than u-shaped, which is a male trait."

"Does it go with either femur?" Booth asked.

"We won't know for sure without further testing,"

Brennan said, shaking her head. "But judging by the epiphysial fusion on the pelvic bones, I'd say the right femur is the more likely candidate as a match for the pelvis . . . and the skull as well."

Picking up the thread as if they had been working together for years, Dr. Wu said, "The cranial sutures are nearly fused—a sign that the skull came from an adult."

"What about race?"

"Judging from the high-bridged nasal bones and narrow face, the skull belongs to a Caucasoid man."

Brennan nodded her agreement. "The bony ridges over the eyes also tell us the skull is that of a man. Plus, we've got both jaws, which gives us something to compare to dental records."

Booth said, "At least two people—one older, one under twenty?"

"Yes," Brennan said. "We'll know more after our exam, but for now . . . let's concentrate on the note."

Booth—eyes brightening like a kid just told to go sit next to the Christmas tree so presents can be handed out—moved closer.

Using her forceps for the second time today, after freshly sterilizing them, Brennan lifted the folded piece of paper from between the skeleton's toes.

She knew better than to use her hands: once they read it, the note would be passed along to the FBI document experts, fingerprint examiners, and trace evidence specialists.

The anthropologist removed the piece of paper, moved it to another table, then—using the forceps and a pointed dental probe borrowed from Dr. Wu— she slowly unfolded the sheet.

It appeared to be a generic piece of white paper, eight and a half by eleven, nothing special . . . until she got it completely open.

The three of them huddled over it.

The letters were from a computer printer, and looked to be a typical font, although Brennan knew very little about such things—basically, she knew enough to type up her reports.

More esoteric uses of the computer were left to her young, brilliant assistant, Zach Addy; or—if it was really difficult, like the 3-D imaging process they could now use to help identify remains—to Angela Montenegro, the lab's true computer whiz.

But it didn't take an expert to see that the note was neatly typed—in all caps and double spaced.

TO THE FBI:

　　I HOPE MY GIFT HAS GOTTEN YOUR AT-
TENTION. I FIND MYSELF NEAR THE END OF
MY CAREER. I HAVE SPENT YEARS OUTSMART-
ING THE LOCALS, BUT THEY HAVE BEEN
UNABLE TO COME ANYWHERE NEAR CAP-

TURING ME. I THINK IT'S TIME TO BRING IN
SOMEONE WHO IS MORE OF A CHALLENGE.
YOUR INVESTIGATION OF THIS PRESENT
WILL SHOW YOU NOT ONLY THAT I HAVE
BEEN AT THIS FOR A WHILE, BUT THAT MY
TARGETS WERE NOT PUSHOVERS. A VICTIM
UNABLE TO DEFEND HIMSELF IS HARDLY A
FAIR TARGET. THOSE BEFORE YOU AND
MANY MORE GAVE THEIR BEST BUT IT WAS
NOT ENOUGH. NONE HAS BEEN ENOUGH.
THE CHALLENGE IS TO YOU, CAN YOU DO
WHAT NONE OF THE VICTIMS AND THE
LOCAL AUTHORITIES HAVE BEEN ABLE TO
DO? CAN YOU STOP ME? COME SEE THE REST
OF MY COLLECTION (IT'S QUITE LARGE) IF
YOU CAN FIND ME.

SAM

"Sam?" Booth asked the air.

Brennan looked from the note to Booth. "I think,"
she said, "you've got a problem."

"You *think*?"

She ignored the sarcasm. "More than one, in fact. If
this 'Sam' is telling the truth, not only have you mis-
placed your star witness . . . you've got a serial killer
on your hands."

Booth pursed his lips. "Maybe he's finally showed
up to do what his *son* couldn't."

"I don't know what that means," Brennan said.

Booth shook his head. "Son of Sam? David Berkowitz? Serial killer, gunned down half a dozen vics, wounded half a dozen more, took instructions from his neighbor's dog? Any of this ring a bell?"

She nodded, eyes narrowed. "Yes. I read a book about it."

The FBI agent looked even more troubled than when he had first shown up at Brennan's hotel room door.

"You all right, Booth?" she asked.

"I don't know," he admitted. "This doesn't look like it's going to lead me to my missing witness."

Brennan blinked. "Is that your only concern?"

He shook his head, chagrined. "Sorry, no. It's just . . . a serial killer is the sort of case that will get my boss to let Musetti go, and drop in *my* lap."

Dr. Wu looked perplexed, but Brennan got it. Booth wasn't being selfish as much as he was considering the unfinished work he, and so many others at the FBI, already had on their collective plate.

And now a completely unrelated task seemed about to be dumped on him.

She thought about her eight-hundred-year-old corpse back in her lab at the Jeffersonian.

And knew how Booth felt.

His poise regained, Booth asked the two scientists, "When do you think you'll have results?"

Brennan and Dr. Wu conferred for a moment.

Brennan said, "We got a late start today. Museum's

closing and my staff at the Jeffersonian will be going home within the hour. By the time we get material to the people who can help us analyze it, we won't have anything before noon tomorrow."

Booth closed his eyes, then a beat later, nodded.

She had figured he would be upset, want results right away like he always did; but now he said nothing, and his expression seemed distracted.

"Are you going to be a while?" he asked her.

"Yeah," she said. "Breaking this skeleton down and figuring out exactly how many people we're dealing with? That'll take most of the night."

"Can you catch a ride back to the hotel?"

Brennan had no idea.

"I'll get her a cab," Dr. Wu said. "It won't be a problem."

Booth said, "Good—that'll give me time to go over the Musetti evidence one more time. My boss'll have gone home for the night, time I get to the office . . . but first thing tomorrow, he's gonna want an update." He sighed. "And that's when Musetti will become a cold case. I've got about twelve hours."

Brennan watched him use her forceps to drop the note into a plastic evidence bag, then turn and go.

In all the times she had worked with Booth, she had never seen him like this. The look of him, though, the way he carried himself, the vacancy in the eyes, *that* she had seen before.

In school the competition for grades had been

fierce, and she had seen this battle-fatigued look from those that were burning out, losing the fight.

This case was eating Booth up, he was losing the fight, and now they might be dealing with a serial killer to boot.

Looking at the skeleton on the table, Brennan knew that Booth might feel he was losing the battle now, but he was not in it alone.

If she could, she would find a way for both of them to win.

3

RIGHT NOW SEELEY BOOTH WANTED TO THROW A punch—not necessarily at a person; a wall would do.

Controlling his temper was something Booth had mastered as a sniper—dispassion was a requisite of the job, and the art—but on days like this, even the limits of a Zen master would be severely tested.

Special Agent in Charge Robert Dillon—Booth's boss on the Musetti/Gianelli case, and head of the Chicago office—had, as Booth had anticipated, ordered him to drop the mob inquiry and concentrate his energy on finding this apparent serial killer with the skeleton calling card.

That more than one body had been used in the construction of the skeleton was enough to convince SAC Dillon that the "apparent" part of that designation was a mere formality: to Dillon (and, truth be known, to Booth) a serial killer was at large in Chicago.

Such a matter had a higher priority than a missing mob rat, who was probably at the bottom of the Chicago River, anyway (or Lake Michigan, or God knew where). Booth understood his superior's thinking. Hell, he would have made the same decision himself, had he been in charge.

But that did not make Booth any more happy as he strode down the hall from Dillon's office, heading for his own and an appointment with a VCR.

He had barely slept four hours.

After leaving Brennan and Dr. Wu at the museum, Booth had returned to the office and sifted through the Musetti evidence until well after midnight.

When he could barely keep his eyes open any longer, he'd driven to his hotel, slept from three until seven, showered, changed clothes, and gotten back in the office by eight.

Dillon had come in not much later and Booth had briefed him on the events of the last twenty-four hours.

Now, having found a cubbyhole of his mind in which to temporarily store Musetti, Booth entered his office, ready to track down this killer. After all, the sooner this madman was behind bars, the sooner Seeley Booth would be back searching for his missing witness.

By the time he had closed his door, loaded the first of the security tapes from the building office, turned on the TV, and dropped into his chair, Booth was as calm as if he had just had an hour-long massage.

The onetime sniper had acquired many skills beyond the one that had been the easiest to learn—marksmanship. Compartmentalizing emotions wasn't just a desire, but a commandment among snipers. An emotional shooter was usually a bad shooter.

He had survived that nastiest of nasty military assignments by finding and developing an ability to be serene, no matter what the surroundings or the circumstance.

Picking up the remote, Booth aimed and squeezed the button.

The tape machine popped to life. The picture on the black-and-white video was grainy and showed the lobby of the Dirksen Building from above and behind the security desk, where Barney, the night guard, sat. The shot was over Barney's head so it was impossible for Booth to tell if the guard was at the desk or not.

The lobby was empty, but what Booth was interested in was beyond the windows. The machine whirred quietly as he watched, his eyes straining to detect any hint of motion outside the building.

In the corner, below the date, the time clicked off one wrenching second at a time, Booth unwilling to fast-forward for fear he would miss something crucial.

He was seven minutes in when a knock at his door almost made him jump—serene or not.

Punching the PAUSE button, Booth said, "What?"

The door opened and Woolfolk framed himself there tentatively.

As usual, the Special Agent's hair was as immaculate as his expression was haggard. His suit was navy blue, shirt light blue, tie a conservative blue stripe, an American flag pin on the left lapel of his jacket.

Booth, who worked hard at looking professional, always felt like the kid with his shirt untucked and his jeans ripped next to Woolfolk.

Yet Woolfolk, easily five years older than Booth, always behaved like he was the kid and the visiting agent from Washington, DC, the old pro.

"What is it?" Booth asked.

The other agent's head dipped a little in deference. "Dillon assigned me to be your wingman on the Skel Case."

Already a nickname for it.

"Pull up a chair," Booth said.

Woolfolk did, and asked, "What are we doing?"

"Right now, we're watching TV."

Booth explained why, then hit PLAY again.

They had been at it about ten minutes when both agents sat forward as a dark figure dragged something into the frame.

The image was so grainy, and they were so far away,

making out what was happening was difficult; but Booth noted the time on the screen's lower corner.

This was their guy, all right.

The figure was dressed head to toe in black, with either a stocking cap or a hooded sweatshirt. The agents weren't seeing any detail from this angle. The skeleton was placed in plain view, the guy moved around it for a few seconds, placing it just right . . .

. . . then was gone.

The whole thing had taken less than twenty seconds.

"So we have him on tape?" Woolfolk asked.

"Not as good as in custody," Booth said with a nod, "but a start."

The tape kept rolling and the night guard, Barney, strolled into frame, then seemed to jump back a little before running out the bottom of the frame, on his way to his desk to call Booth. Five minutes of less than riveting security-cam "action" later, both Booth and Barney crossed into the frame and went outside.

"That's enough," Booth said. "Put in the next tape."

Woolfolk did as he was told.

This tape was an exterior angle, the security camera mounted on the side of the building, shooting down toward Plymouth Square. Booth fast-forwarded to a few seconds before the suspect appeared.

There their litterer was, dropping the skeleton in

front of the building and spreading out the extremities, then trotting away.

This time, though, the agents saw him disappear around a corner.

Booth hit rewind and they watched it again—specifically, the skeleton being set down and spread out.

Booth pointed at the screen. "Did you see that?"

"See what?" Woolfolk asked, leaning forward, squinting at the image.

"*There*," Booth said, rewinding again. He played a few seconds and paused the tape, the suspect reaching out to straighten the skeleton's arm.

"I don't know what I'm supposed to see," Woolfolk said.

"Right *there*," Booth said, rising, pointing at the screen.

"Right where?"

Moving around the desk, Booth pointed to the suspect's arm. "His sleeve pulled up away from the glove. That white spot is his arm. He's Caucasian."

Woolfolk nodded. "Yeah, *yeah*—I see it."

Booth made a face. "Really narrowing the suspect list, huh?"

"Gotta start somewhere," Woolfolk said with a shrug.

They played the tape a couple more times, but gained no new insights. Through the series of tapes from other buildings and traffic lights, they managed to track the suspect's movements from three blocks away to the Dirksen Building, then back.

In the end, though, the perp always rounded a corner and disappeared.

And none of the views showed them much more than a figure in black—the only significant upgrade was ruling out the stocking cap and identifying the perp's headgear as the hood of a sweatshirt.

"Where the hell did he *go*?" Woolfolk asked.

Booth rewound the tape, played it again, rewound it, played it, and then again.

Finally, he said, "Tapes don't tell us, and I don't have a guess."

"Well, he had to go *somewhere*."

They watched various tapes several more times.

"Somewhere around that building," Woolfolk said, pointing to an ornately styled structure at the corner of Adams and LaSalle.

In the paused black-and-white video, Booth knew the other agent couldn't see the burnt orange masonry that made the building easy to identify, even if you weren't an architectural buff, or a local.

"The Rookery," he said.

"Why have I heard of that?" Woolfolk asked.

"You work in downtown Chicago, you oughta have."

"I didn't grow up here, Seeley. I've only been in this post since February."

Booth leaned back in his chair and cast a condescending smile at his new partner. In his best tour guide voice, he spoke.

"The Rookery sits on the site of the temporary city hall after the Chicago Fire. Place used to draw a lot of pigeons. When the building went up, it got dubbed 'the Rookery' and the name took. Home office of architects Daniel Burnham and John W. Root, who designed any number of famous buildings in the city."

Woolfolk's tired eyes had woken up. "How in the hell do you know that?"

Booth shrugged. "Kind of an architecture buff. Wanted to be one when I was a kid."

"Somehow I didn't see you as an architect."

"Yeah, and that's how it worked out; but it's a great field—all about turning something in your head into something real, something that can shelter people . . . a building, a home."

Woolfolk pondered that, then said, "Maybe it's not that different from what we do."

Booth had never made a connection and said so.

Woolfolk explained. "We look at evidence and keep arranging the pieces until they suggest a picture; and we work our asses off taking this abstract idea we have, and turning it into something concrete enough to catch a bad guy . . . and put him away."

Booth chuckled. "Josh, you have depths I never dreamed of."

Woolfolk summoned a rumpled grin. "Same back at

you. So what picture are you assembling in your mind, Seeley, from this grainy video?"

Booth gestured toward the frozen image on the screen. "Suspect disappears ... either inside the Rookery, which should have been locked up at that time of night ... or down an alley or manhole or ... something."

"Next step?"

"Find me more videotape from that area, the Rookery's security video, and interview their night guard."

Woolfolk was already on his feet. "And what will you be up to?"

"I've got to check in with our science squints at the museum, and see if they've come up with anything on the skeleton. . . . When I get back, we'll start finding anything we can about missing men and serial killers in the area, particularly the variety that challenges the authorities to catch them."

"Roger that," Woolfolk said.

"Remember, sooner we catch this guy, sooner we're back on Musetti."

With a quick nod, Woolfolk slipped out.

When Booth arrived at the Field Museum, he had to wait for an employee to escort him through all the locked doors until he once more found himself in the basement with Dr. Wu and Brennan.

If the anthropologists hadn't changed their clothes,

Booth might have thought they'd been down here all night.

Brennan looked crisp and fresh in black slacks and a gray blouse. Dr. Wu wore gray slacks and a blue sleeveless turtleneck and appeared equally alert.

Booth gave the doctor a big smile, which she returned.

"Good morning, Dr. Wu—Bones. What do we know?"

Brennan raised both eyebrows and her smile wasn't exactly a smile. "We know for starters that calling me 'Bones' gets the day off to a bad start."

"Sorry," Booth said halfheartedly.

Dr. Wu folded her arms. "*Sherlock* Bones would be more like it—with all the detective work she's been doing since you saw her last."

Booth grinned and Brennan's smile morphed into a real one.

Back to business, Booth asked, "So, what can you tell me about our skeletal door prize?"

Dr. Wu glanced at Brennan, who led them closer to the worktable.

The skeleton had been cut apart, its puppet strings snipped and all the connecting wires in a pile on the next table over; on this surface, the bones were laid out in the form of the body.

"Why cut the wires?" Booth asked, his instinct being that evidence should be preserved.

"All strung up like a Christmas turkey," Brennan said, "it was hard to examine."

She gestured to the pile nearby.

"We saved the wires and were careful to wear gloves while we handled them," she said. "My guess is they're clean of prints, but you should send them to your lab, of course. Maybe they'll get lucky."

"Done," Booth said.

Brennan's eyebrows raised again. "As for the remains themselves? You knew already that the femora told us there were at least two different bodies."

"Yeah. Playing at being one."

"Right," Dr. Wu said. "And now we're pretty sure you can double your total."

"Four sources?" Booth asked, goggling at the display of bones. "We have potentially four victims here?"

Brennan raised a cautionary palm. "We won't know for sure until we get the results of more tests. . . ."

Dr. Wu completed the thought: "But the preliminary evidence has us leaning that way."

The two women exchanged glances and nods.

Surprised, Booth said, "Bones, *you* don't 'lean.' You're all about empirical evidence. If you can't prove it, you don't believe it."

Brennan said, "I knew you would want as much as we could give you . . . so I'm pushing the envelope a little."

He just stared at her.

She gestured toward the skeletal remains. "Here—look at the vertebrae."

Booth leaned in. "The spine?"

"*Most* of it," Brennan said. "The top seven are the cervical vertebrae, next twelve are the thoracic vertebrae, and then there are five lumbar vertebrae above the sacrum and coccyx."

"Okay," Booth said, not knowing where she was going with this anatomy lesson.

"For the time being, ignore the lumbar vertebrae on down."

No problem, he thought. He had been ignoring most of this stuff since college. *Including* college. . . .

"The seven cervical vertebrae," Brennan was saying, "are all from the same body."

"At least we *think* they are," Dr. Wu put in.

"Yes," Brennan said, and her head tilted to one side and the palm came up again. "Pending further *tests*. . . . But they fit together as if they belong together—you understand?"

He shrugged.

"The wear patterns are consistent within those seven bones. They fit together as if they've been working together for a long time."

Booth considered that. "Like a nut and bolt that have been together for years?"

Dr. Wu said, "Exactly. You put on a new nut and it

doesn't tighten down exactly the same . . . but if you put the old one back on, voilà, fits perfectly."

He nodded and the Field expert smiled at him again.

They really seemed to be hitting it off. Was she flirting with him? Guys were supposed to know when women were flirting, but Booth could never really sort through the signals.

Tessa, a lawyer he had been seeing, practically threw herself at him before he figured it out. Coming out of his little reverie, he noticed Brennan smirking at him.

"What?" he asked defensively.

"Nothing," she said, in that tone that always meant "nothing" was something. "Are you listening?"

"Of course I'm listening!"

Brennan returned her attention to the skeleton, pointing as she spoke. "What is true of the cervical vertebrae is true of the twelve thoracic vertebrae as well. They fit together like they belong . . . and again, the wear patterns seem consistent with them coming from the same body."

"Hold on," Booth said. "The cervicals and thoracics came from the same body?"

Brennan said, "Yes and no. The cervical vertebrae are all from one body; and the thoracic vertebrae are from one body—they just happen to be two *different* bodies."

"Does your head hurt? My head hurts."

"I feel fine," Brennan said.

A concerned Dr. Wu asked Booth, "Would you like some aspirin?"

Booth waved that off, bobbing his head toward the skeletal "corpse" and saying, "Cervical from one, thoracic from the other. And neither of them are from the other two?"

Brennan nodded. "Wear on the thoracic vertebrae shows that the person they belong to had something wrong with one of his legs—causing the vertebrae to wear unevenly and in a way that is not normal."

Brennan pointed to the worn areas.

"See these edges?" she asked. "They should have worn more evenly. Although the intervertebral disks are gone, you can see where they were worn down, and the surfaces of the vertebrae started rubbing against each other. Whatever was wrong with his leg caused him to hurt his back and any movement—especially walking—would have been extremely painful."

"What was wrong with his leg?" Booth asked.

Dr. Wu said, "Could have been any number of things."

"For instance?"

"Slipped femoral epiphysis would have done the trick."

"Slipped what?" Booth said.

Brennan pointed to the ends of the femora. "Remember when we told you about the epiphysis sutures closing to show age?"

"Sure."

"Well, this is the same area—the epiphysial cap on the femoral head." Brennan pointed. "If the epiphysis slips out, the leg will rotate laterally."

She turned the femur away from the body.

"The foot would have been turned out," she continued. "Walking would have put torque and stress on the spine."

Dr. Wu said, "The leg could have been broken and not set—could've been torture, or a birth defect that was never dealt with . . . lots of possible explanations."

"Bottom line?" Booth asked.

"Bottom line," Dr. Wu said, "is both of these femora are healthy . . . and if that's what caused the wear on the spine, then the thoracic vertebrae could not possibly have come from this skeleton."

"Okay," Booth said, and heaved his biggest sigh of the day—so far. "Then we've got at least three victims."

Brennan said, "The cervical vertebrae come from a body that was dead for a lot longer than either femur . . . and probably longer than the thoracic vertebrae as well. Though, of course, we—"

"Need more tests," Booth interrupted.

"That's right."

Booth gestured toward the skeleton again. "What about the cervical vertebrae?"

"First," Brennan said, in a little too teacherly a way for Booth's taste, "you need to understand that skeletal decomposition can be broken down into rough stages."

"All right," Booth said.

"In the first stage, the bones are greasy and decomposed tissue remains." She pointed, demonstrating. "That's what most of these bones are."

"Got it."

"In the next stage, the bones still retain some mummified or putrefied tissue, but covering less than half of the skeleton."

He nodded.

"In stage three the bones have lost all tissue and some organic components, but may retain a slight greasiness. The thoracic vertebrae and some of the foot bones indicate this. The bones are completely dry by stage four; the cervical vertebrae have signs of this stage and the next, which is when the bones are dry with bleaching and exfoliation. In the sixth stage, the dry bones show increased deterioration with metaphyseal loss and cancellous exposure; but we don't have any bones that are that far gone."

"So," Booth asked, "the cervical vertebrae are the oldest?"

"Yes," Brennan said. "I'd say this victim has been dead for as long as . . ." She glanced at Dr. Wu, who nodded. ". . . forty years."

Booth whistled. "Back in the sixties?"

"Possible. Very possible."

"Is it also possible that someone used real bones but faked all this—you know, doctored these things— just to screw with us?"

Shaking her head, Dr. Wu said, "I think we've eliminated that—you've got bones here that would not just be lying around. Forty-year-old cervical vertebrae are not like finding an Indian arrowhead in a state park."

Her cell phone rang and Dr. Wu said, "Excuse me."

She took the phone off her belt, touched a button, and said, "Jane Wu." She listened for a few seconds, said, "I'll be right there," and clicked off.

"I'm sorry," she said to Brennan. "Crisis upstairs. Be back as soon as I can."

Brennan and Booth both nodded and Dr. Wu left, Booth watching the attractive way she walked as she went.

Turning his attention back to Brennan—who was smirking at him again—he said, "So, you two are saying I've got a serial killer who has been at it for *forty years*?"

"I know it sounds far-fetched," Brennan said, all business. "But that's where the evidence is leading us."

A geriatric killer?

The killer taunting Booth would have to be, what? Sixty years old, at least?

Booth's stomach knotted. This was not going to go over well with his boss.

Brennan said, "The note indicated this . . ." She

gestured toward the table of remains. ". . . was a good-bye gesture of sorts. So we shouldn't be surprised. Right?"

"You mentioned more tests," Booth said, ignoring the question. "What's that involve?"

"Taking the remains to the Jeffersonian so my staff can do DNA, track the dental records . . . assuming the skull is from the same person, which it might be. And we'll have Angela do a holographic reconstruction." She smiled at him. "You know, 'squint' stuff."

"How long will that take?" he asked, blowing past her friendly dig.

"Going to take a while," she admitted. "But the sooner we get going, the better."

"We?" he asked, afraid he knew where this was heading. "You don't mean *you* and *me*, do you?"

"No," she retorted. "The skeleton and me . . . That 'we.' The sooner *we* get going to Washington, the sooner *I* can call you with the results."

"You're . . . going back?"

She nodded. "Sure, why not? You don't need me here. The work is the skeleton, and the skeleton needs to be in DC."

Though he could not say why, Booth suddenly felt uneasy, and queasy. They were in this together. They were . . . God, he wasn't going to admit it to himself was he? . . . a team.

"You just got here," he said, knowing it sounded lame even before the words tumbled out.

She eyed him with sublime condescension. "And it's been wonderful . . . but I need to go where the work takes me."

"Yeah," he said, lowering his head. "You're right, of course."

Brennan jerked a thumb toward the table of bones. "When Dr. Wu gets back, we'll package up the remains and I'll be ready to go."

He nodded.

"Think you can book me a flight on such short notice?"

Hauling out his cell phone, he said, "I'll get someone at my office right on it."

"Good. Thanks."

"You know me, Bones. Whatever you need."

Five minutes later, he had explained the problem to one of the agents in his office, who was working on it. He dropped the phone back in his pocket and waited for the call.

He looked over at Brennan, who was already packaging up the bones of the feet, packing them carefully in cotton and placing them in a cardboard box that would be her carry-on when she got to the airport.

Booth wondered why he felt the need for her to stay. They had no personal life together at all; they were, for the most part, oil and water—calling them "friendly" would be a stretch, though "friends" somehow wasn't.

So, what the hell was the problem?

He shook his head, forcing the thoughts away.

The *problem* was a serial killer—a geezer of a one, perhaps—but a serial killer nonetheless, and by definition dangerous as hell.

If Bones was right, this was a fiend who had not been caught in the course of a forty-year career in which he (or possibly she) had killed at least four people and probably a lot more.

Dr. Wu returned and Booth watched as the two scientists finished prepping and packing the remains.

They had just finished when Booth's cell phone chirped. The agent on the line gave him Brennan's travel information.

"Got you on a United flight leaving at nine," Booth told her.

Brennan glanced at her watch. "That should be fine—thanks. I need you to stop by the hotel to pick up my bag, of course."

"Of course."

Booth's intention had been to call a car for her and get back to work; but she had obviously made the judgment that Booth was her ride to the airport, and he decided now was not the time to rock that particular boat.

He simply nodded and Brennan went back to talking to Dr. Wu.

Least you can do, he told himself.

After all, he had dragged her to Chicago and had

not been on hand to meet her when she arrived. He'd better see her off, or there would be hell to pay at some point.

Women never forgot things like that, in Booth's experience, and men usually didn't even know they were supposed to remember them.

But Booth knew this much: Brennan was helping him, and he needed to reciprocate, out of professional courtesy, if nothing else.

Brennan picked up the box and Booth took a step toward her, but she shook her head. She had it, and his trying to help would be misconstrued. She would believe that he was thinking he was stronger, and should therefore carry the box for her.

Okay, so she wouldn't *really* be misconstruing his thought process—just the reasoning behind it. Wasn't that he thought she was weak: he just liked to help people, even science squints who felt they had to prove their worth every second.

Dr. Wu handed him her card. "If you have any questions, Special Agent Booth, anything at all, feel free to give me a call."

He accepted the card, the doctor's hand brushing against his.

He smiled at her, grateful for any friendly gesture from an attractive female.

She returned the smile. "Call anytime. My home number is on the back."

"I appreciate that."

Brennan, fairly testy, said, "This box isn't getting any lighter. . . ."

Shaking hands with Dr. Wu, Booth said, "Thank you for everything. The Field's been most hospitable."

"Our pleasure," she said, but to Booth it sounded like *My pleasure*. . . .

Over by the door, Brennan let out a little *harumph* and Booth ran to get the door for her. His mind was whirling with what was correct to do for a modern female, and what wasn't. . . .

At the car, he opened the trunk and she set the box inside. She got in on the passenger side before he had time to work out whether he should risk getting it for her or not.

Soon Booth was battling his way through Lake Shore Drive traffic on his way back to her hotel. The ride passed in relative silence, driver and passenger lost in thought, Booth mulling how the hell he was going to track down a killer about whom he knew next to nothing. . . .

Parking the Crown Vic under the hotel's canopy, Booth got out, flashed his ID at the valet, and said, "Official business. Leave it here. We'll be back soon."

The valet, realizing there would be no tip, nodded at Booth and looked away.

As he followed Brennan up to her room, Booth sifted the pieces of what he knew.

The suspect who had delivered the skeleton was white. Was he the killer or just an accomplice?

Brennan and Dr. Wu thought they had parts of four people—all victims of the killer?

One of the source bodies for the skeleton had been dead for over forty years—an old victim, or a piece robbed from a grave to throw them off?

As the anthropologist packed her bag, one thing was clear to Booth: he had no shortage of questions . . . just a surfeit of answers.

Well, maybe Brennan and her squint squad could come up with something back at the Jeffersonian. He felt tired, bone-tired (appropriately enough), and it didn't look like he'd be catching up on sleep anytime soon.

Brennan checked out and they put her duffel in the trunk alongside the box of bones, and Booth got them on the expressway toward O'Hare Airport.

After a few minutes of silence, Brennan asked, "Are you going to ask her out?"

The question took Booth by surprise. "Ask who what?"

Though she said nothing, he could feel her eyes on him. He took it as long as he could before he turned to look at her.

"Dr. Wu," Brennan said. Her voice and her face were expressionless, her tone equally blank. "I know I'm not the best person at picking up signals, but even I could tell she was practically throwing herself at you."

"Well, if so, I missed it," Booth claimed, not even convincing himself . . .

. . . although it didn't feel bad, having Brennan corroborate his theory.

Brennan stared straight ahead.

"I dunno." He shrugged. "Maybe you're right. Maybe I should give her a call."

"*I'm* right?" Brennan rolled her eyes, and then seemed to burrow down farther in her seat.

"Want to get something to eat?" Booth asked her. "There's time before your flight."

"Not hungry."

They lapsed back into silence.

Booth was entering the serpentine access to the airport, when his cell phone chirped in his pocket.

"Booth."

"Woolfolk. God, I'm glad I caught you."

The agent was breathless.

Booth frowned. "What?"

Booth listened as the other agent spoke.

When Woolfolk finally stopped, Booth could only manage two words, "Oh Christ."

He clicked off and turned to Brennan, who frowned, clearly not liking the lines she'd been reading between.

"No bones are going on that flight today," he told her glumly. "Not you . . . and not that box in the trunk, either. . . ."

4

TEMPERANCE BRENNAN'S IRRITATION EXISTED ON dual levels—neither one, she knew, particularly rational.

She wasn't exactly jealous over Booth's saying he might call Dr. Jane Wu. That, after all, was none of her business. And why should she care?

After all, they had no real relationship beyond work, had never dated, never even gone out for a drink together....

Okay, so the handsome FBI agent in her novel, *Bred in the Bone*, had borne a greater likeness to Booth than she had intended. In her mind, Booth had been in the mix, the fictional agent a composite of Booth, several other agents, and her imagination.

When her staff had called her on the character's being Booth-And-Only-Booth, she had pooh-poohed the idea; but Angela—whose mission was to fix people up with each other and make everybody and everything happy and nice—had jumped all over it, despite Brennan's protestations.

If Brennan found herself rolling her eyes over Booth's knee-jerk response to the attractive Dr. Wu, her own knee-jerk response, about someone she had on occasion worked with, only made her shake her head . . . at herself.

If forced, she'd have described her relationship with Booth as more of . . . a brother and sister thing (to which Angela would not doubt gibe, "Right—like in the Ozarks!"). Even if she felt the feelings Angela attributed to her, however, Brennan knew such a relationship would be unprofessional; and professionalism was as close to a personal code as Brennan had thus far formed.

Besides, she was not in the right place in her life for any kind of male-female connection.

What bothered her most, though, were her envious feelings about Dr. Wu. The Field Museum anthropologist—whom Brennan liked and respected—saw what she wanted and went right after it, an approach that had always been out of reach for Brennan . . . at least when it came to male-female stuff.

Envying someone for having the self-assurance to strive for what she wanted, well, that irked Brennan—about herself. Envy seemed petty. *Was* petty, she knew.

That didn't make the feeling go away.

She neither liked nor trusted such feelings. As a scientist, she preferred an intellectual path. "Feelings" were nothing more than emotion, a desire for something that the brain told you was probably counterproductive.

Just minutes ago, this frustration had seemed about to reach a blessed conclusion. She'd be on a flight back to DC with the remains, and Agent Seeley Booth would be half a continent away.

She'd sat in Booth's Crown Vic, looking out the window, ignoring the man behind the wheel, relieved to see the WELCOME TO O'HARE AIRPORT sign as they started up the serpentine road that led to the terminal.

But then Booth's cell phone chirped, and everything changed.

"What do you mean," she said, trying not to sound as irritated (and frustrated) as she felt, "I'm not going on that flight?"

These were the first words she had spoken to him in quite a while.

Sitting behind the wheel at the curb, with the motor running, he appeared lost in thought, and his response had an absent quality: "Guess we'll have to FedEx the skeleton."

"What kind of silly red tape have you got us caught up in? Booth, I take stuff like that on planes with me all the *time*!"

As he turned to her now, she could see Booth's troubled expression, the angles of his face highlighted by the setting sun.

"You won't be able to convey that evidence," he explained, "because you won't be getting on that plane."

"Why the hell not?"

He tasted his tongue; didn't seem to care for the flavor. "Because we need you . . . *I* need you."

"Be still, my beating heart," she said. "*Why* do you need me?"

"Seems we just got ourselves another skeleton."

". . . Another . . ." She gaped at him. "You have to be—" But she didn't complete that: he clearly *wasn't* "kidding."

He flipped the switch for the flashing lights and got the car in gear and the siren going.

Gunning the car and dodging around a taxi, he said, "Call just came in—skel number two, outside a theater in Old Town."

"Old Town?"

They were speeding now, headed back toward the expressway. "On the North Side, border of Old Town and Wrigleyville, two sections of the city."

"You seem to know your way around Chicago pretty well. . . ."

He zoomed past a truck, jumped two lanes left. "Feels like I've been here forever, on this mob case. But I spent some time in the Windy City when I was a kid, yeah."

Oddly, a part of her didn't mind staying, while a more sensible portion of her mind was frustrated that her evidence would head home without her.

Finally she asked, "This . . . new skeleton?"

"Yeah?"

"Wired together, like the last one?"

"Don't know—my guy Woolfolk didn't say—you know as much as I do."

They rode in silence for a time, cars barely getting out of their way or forcing Booth to swerve around them.

Brennan worked at remaining calm, and on the outside it took; but inside, despite having dug up mass graves during wars in Bosnia, Guatemala, and half a dozen other hellholes, she felt something approaching apprehension.

They were hurtling through traffic to get to a skeleton, a dead person, someone who could not get up and walk away . . . and yet Booth was racing there like they could arrive and perform CPR on the patient.

"Why?" he asked, with a sideways glance.

The word, after all that silence, seemed a non sequitur.

She squinted at him. "Why what?"

"Why do you want to know if our new skeleton is wired?"

Glad to have something to think about besides imminent death in a car crash, Brennan pondered the question.

"Just—the timing," she said at last.

"How's the timing relate?"

"Well, it's just now getting dark. What's the neighborhood like around that theater?"

Booth considered. "Lots of shops, restaurants, bars, apartments above businesses."

Brennan nodded. "No shortage of traffic—foot and car both."

"Plenty."

"Daylight, or near to it, lots of traffic . . . and your suspect managed to drop a skeleton right in front of a theater?"

"Not in *front* of the theater," Booth clarified. "Actually in an alley next to the building . . . but I get your point. Reasonable to assume *some* passerby would notice a guy lugging around a skeleton, or even a big unwieldy package."

Her eyes narrowed. "The remains are in an alley?"

"Yeah. A famous alley, at that."

"How does an alley get 'famous'?"

"John Dillinger gets shot in it."

"The bank robber from the thirties," she said, eyes narrowing further.

"July 22, 1934, to be exact—Melvin Purvis and a squad of FBI agents shot Dillinger dead in an alley outside the Biograph Theater."

"The FBI—it doesn't go back much further than that, does it?"

"No. It was just this fledgling agency called the Division of Investigation. Purvis taking Dillinger down was a big deal—a public relations coup for the bureau."

". . . Don't you see, Booth?"

"See what?"

"You're being taunted. This killer is thumbing his nose at the Federal Bureau of Investigation."

Booth frowned. "You could be right."

"You mean, I *am* right."

His eyes were on the traffic, and his response came so late, Brennan almost didn't know what he meant.

"You are right," he said.

Almost didn't know what he meant. . . .

The neighborhood turned out to be as Booth had indicated—considerable foot traffic going by the shops, bars, and of course the famous theater (sadly closed but with its marquee promising to "reopen soon" with performances by the Victory Gardens theater company).

At the moment, pedestrians were forced to cross to the other side of the street, police having put up crime scene tape to cordon off the area of the alley and around the theater.

As Booth double-parked, Brennan could see the passersby gawking at the scene—police and federal agents milling around the mouth of the alley, haphazardly parked cars both marked and unmarked, the coroner's van closest to the alley.

Booth displayed his ID, sticking it into his breast

pocket. The cops cleared a path and Brennan followed, ducking under the crime scene tape as they entered the dark alley.

Night had settled over the city and their path was illuminated by halogen work lights, two to a yellow tripod, the tripods set every ten feet or so along the alley, with a triangle of them pointed at something on the ground at the far end.

Three men in suits waited there as well, talking to each other, watching as she and Booth approached.

As they neared these men, Brennan could see that the closest one stood up straight, his square shoulders back, chest out, his expensive suit barely able to contain his alpha male attitude.

He was definitely the boss.

Booth said, "Special Agent in Charge Robert Dillon, this is the anthropologist I told you about—Dr. Temperance Brennan."

Dillon extended his hand. "Glad to have you aboard, Dr. Brennan."

As she shook his hand, she struggled to keep her face impassive. Welcome aboard? As if they were fellow passengers on a cruise ship? He had a firm grip, and dark eyes that struck her as avian and predatory.

But his next remark was friendly enough: "Your reputation precedes you."

"Thank you. I never expected to be doing anthropological work on the streets of Chicago."

"And we never dreamed we'd have to ask you to."

He turned to a tall man of thirty-five or so with stubbly brown hair, a day's growth of beard, a strong chin, lively brown eyes, and an affable expression that nonetheless told Brennan he was checking her out . . . and not for her professional expertise.

Dillon said, "This is Lieutenant Brett Greene of the Chicago PD."

Greene extended his hand. He wore black slacks, an open-collared black shirt, and black leather coat. "Nice to meet you, Dr. Brennan."

She shook his hand, a warm, friendly handshake that matched his expression.

"You, too," she said, giving him a professional smile.

Booth introduced the third man. "This is Special Agent Josh Woolfolk. He's my partner on this investigation."

Brennan felt vaguely hurt by that—wasn't she Booth's partner?

Smaller and older than Booth, Woolfolk might have been a middle manager, with his well-kept dark hair swept over to the right, wearing a light blue shirt and darker blue tie under a navy suit.

She shook his hand, said hello, and then looked toward the object under the triangle of work lights.

Brennan had expected a skeleton similar to the last one, but what she saw was a garbage bag with the top open. From here, she could not see the bag's contents.

"What have we got?" Booth asked.

Despite the presence of the federal agents, the Chicago cop, Greene, spoke up. "Homeless guy saw somebody dump this garbage bag back here."

Greene squatted next to the bag and carefully held the top open so they could look inside.

A skull and a pile of bones beneath it.

Greene said, "Homeless guy says that he thought there might be good trash in there . . . these scavengers check everything out . . . so he opened the bag." Greene laughed. "When he saw the bones, he freaked. Ran back to the street and flagged down a squad car."

"Where's our witness now?" Booth asked.

Greene jerked his head toward the street. "Backseat of a squad."

Crouching next to Booth, hands on her knees, Brennan peered into the bag that Greene still held open.

Under the harsh glare of the work lights, the skull was white—bleached-looking. She also saw at least one femur, both humeri, ribs, two tibiae, and a pile of smaller bones.

No wire this time, but what seemed to be a complete human skeleton.

Again.

"We need to get this to the Field Museum," she said.

Dillon checked his watch. "Closed by now."

Brennan glanced up at Booth. "Call Jane Wu. Use her home number, if you have to—I mean, you *do* have it. . . ."

Booth gave her a funny look, but said, "Good idea."

"Wu who?" Dillon asked.

Greene smiled at that, his eyes catching Brennan's.

"*Dr.* Wu," Booth said to his superior. "Our contact at the Field Museum—also an anthropologist."

"Call her, by all means," Dillon said.

"But before you go poking around in this bag," Greene said, holding up a traffic-cop palm, "it goes to the station to be printed."

Brennan nodded. "I have no problem with that."

The three federal officers gave her a collective fish eye.

"Well, isn't that the next logical step?" she asked, looking at Booth. "Fingerprinting the bag and its contents?"

Dillon answered crisply. "We don't generally take orders from local officers."

Shrugging, Brennan asked, "I'm just a consultant, on only one aspect of this investigation . . . but if I might suggest? Why don't we table any turf wars, and just work together on this—we might get farther, faster."

Dillon frowned but said nothing.

Brennan turned away from the federal agent and

faced Lieutenant Greene. "You'll have that done tonight and the bones will be at the Field Museum first thing in the morning, right?"

Greene had been grinning when Brennan had the heat on Dillon, but now that it was on him, the smile faded. "Yeah, sure, no problem, only—"

"You need the address of the museum?"

Again, the detective looked uncomfortable. "No, I know where the Field Museum is! Jeez."

"Good. Where's the nearest FedEx?"

Greene told her, then said to the others, "I'm all for the cooperation Dr. Brennan advises; but this body, bones or not, was found in a Chicago alley. I don't see what makes it a federal matter."

Dillon said, "The first skeleton was found on government property, the Dirksen Building—this is clearly the same perp, and the same case."

"Do we *know* that?" Greene asked.

"Come on, Lieutenant," Dillon said. "You saw the note addressed to us. . . . Now, take the bag and the remains. We'll take this." He pulled a plastic evidence bag out of his pocket. "And we'll make sure it gets to Quantico ASAP."

"What have you got there, Robert?" Booth asked.

It was Woolfolk who answered, chiming in, "Another note, Booth."

Booth glared at Dillon. "Little slow telling me, don't you think?"

"Just hadn't got around to it," his superior said, unapologetic.

Brennan didn't know whether to laugh or cry at all this male posturing; and would it have happened if she weren't here, she wondered? The answer to that question seemed obvious to an anthropologist.

Dillon was saying, "Let's get back to the car."

Brennan trailed the men back up the alley, the crime scene investigators passing them as they made their way back to the homeless man's discovery.

As the little group neared the cars, Brennan saw another man she didn't know, but undeniably a federal agent, using a digital camera to snap photos of the crowd of gawkers behind the crime scene tape, lined up three and four deep.

Watching him photograph the people reminded Brennan of something she had heard about serial killers—that they sometimes inserted themselves into the investigation, so they could find out what the authorities knew, and give themselves the rush of power that came with knowing how close they were to getting caught.

And relishing a sense of power was a part of every serial killer's psyche. . . .

She looked out at the faces—young, old, Caucasian, African-American, Hispanic, Asian, eyes looking back at her, past her, glancing left, peering right.

Was the killer out there?

He—or she—could be any one of them or none of them. No way to tell by just looking. And, anyway, Brennan always found the dead more cooperative than the living. . . .

Booth, Dillon, Woolfolk, and Greene formed a small circle between two unmarked cars. Brennan strolled over, Woolfolk and Greene separating to make room for her.

Woolfolk held a small MagLite that he turned on when Dillon spread out the note.

Even through the plastic evidence bag, it was easy to read:

TO THE FBI:

I CAN'T WAIT FOREVER, THE CLOCK IS TICKING. YOU'LL HAVE TO DO BETTER THAN THE LOCAL COPS EVER DID. THEY HAVE HAD MULTIPLE CHANCES TO STOP ME AND HAVE FAILED. I GIVE YOU ANOTHER GIFT FROM MY COLLECTION TO SHOW YOU THAT I AM SERIOUS.

THERE ARE MANY PLACES TO FIND MALE VICTIMS, MANY OF THEM IN THIS VERY NEIGHBORHOOD. I THOUGHT IT BEST TO BRING YOU CLOSER TO MY TURF. TIME IS OF THE ESSENCE. LOOK HARD, MY NEW FRIENDS, I'M EVERYWHERE, YOU SHOULD HAVE NO TROUBLE FINDING ME.

I'LL BE WAITING,

TIM

"Tim?" Booth asked. "What the hell happened to *Sam?"*

"Sam?" Greene asked.

"That's how the first note was signed," Booth said.

"What first note?" the Chicago cop asked.

Brennan watched as Booth's eyes cut to Dillon.

"A similar note was attached to the skeleton at the Dirksen Building," Dillon said. "We'll send you a copy."

"A copy?" Greene blurted. "Take your time, no rush—it's just evidence in a series of goddamn murders! Are you going to take Dr. Brennan's advice and work with us on this, or *what?"*

Dillon kept his voice low, his face impassive, but his tone had an edge.

"Lieutenant Greene," he said, "get a grip. We have a crowd around, including media, and God only knows how many with cameras—is this what you want broadcast? That we're *not* cooperating?"

Greene started to say something, glanced around, then blew out a long breath. "Okay . . . you have a point. But the alley by the Biograph is not federal property."

"Be that as it may," Dillon said, "the first skeleton *was* found on federal property. Anyway, at the time, we didn't know if the note was credible or just a diversion."

Greene blinked. "Diversion?"

"We weren't sure what that skeleton represented, Lieutenant. Whether we had a prank, or a murder—that's part of why we flew Dr. Brennan in from DC. Here on out, we'll keep you up to speed, Lieutenant—you have my word."

"All right," Greene relented. "Do that, and there'll be no more bitching on my end. You'll keep us in the loop on the notes, we'll deal with the other physical evidence. . . . Now, tell me, for Christ sake—who the hell is *Sam*?"

Booth said, "Like I said—it's how the killer signed the first note. Now we've got 'Tim' claiming the work."

Greene's brow furrowed. "The other note looked similar?"

"At first blush," Booth said, "the work of the same correspondent."

Greene's wheels were turning. "Son of Sam reference, you think?"

Shrugging, Booth said, "That occurred to me, too. But honestly, I don't know. Maybe he's signing the name of another noted serial killer to each note. . . . Anybody know a serial killer named Tim?"

Woolfolk said, "There was that guy—Judy."

"Judy? We're looking for a Tim."

"Steven *Timothy* Judy. Guy raped and killed women in Indiana, Texas, Louisiana, and California. Eleven in all, including drowning three children of one of his victims."

Greene offered, "There's Timothy McVeigh." The man convicted for the bombing of the Murrah Building in Oklahoma City in 1995.

"Not really a serial," Booth pointed out.

Brennan said, "If he's taunting you, invoking someone who struck at the federal government before could be part of that."

Dillon's eyes were on her. "Taunting us?"

Booth said, "Dr. Brennan has the idea, and I think it's a good one, that the choice of this site has to do with the Dillinger shooting."

Greene laughed. "That's ridiculous. . . . Sorry, Doc, but that's—"

"No," Dillon said. "She's right again—this was the site of one of the Bureau's first great triumphs . . . nailing Public Enemy Number One."

Booth nodded. "The guy is definitely yankin' our chain."

Dillon, his scowl deeper than usual, said, "Let's yank *his*, shall we?"

"Yes, sir." Booth turned to Greene. "I'd like a chat with our homeless citizen."

"No problem," Greene said.

Dillon put a hand on Booth's shoulder. "I'll be calling it a day—Seeley, it's all yours from here."

"Thanks, Robert. I've got it."

Dillon got in his unmarked car and started the engine. They watched him navigate through the thinning crowd into traffic.

The bystanders were losing interest—no one could see what was in the alley, and the coroner's van had pulled away empty. No blood, no further excitement, no reason for them to hang around. Time to head for dinner or home.

Woolfolk brandished the note in the evidence bag, said, "I'll get on this," and was gone as well.

Greene led Booth and Brennan to an unmarked car up the block. The detective opened the back door and made a motioning gesture. A tall, older man unfolded himself from the backseat.

Brennan was surprised to see the man's hands cuffed behind his back.

Rail-thin, the man wore a threadbare black suit several sizes too big for him, a shirt that had once been white with a Superman tee shirt pulled over, and grimy tennis shoes.

Brennan was estimating the man had not bathed in weeks when a shift in breeze confirmed her theory.

Their homeless gent had a receding hairline, a gray beard, and a wad of nose that seemed to take up most of his face. The scruffy visage was softened, however, by mild blue eyes.

"Why is he cuffed?" Booth asked. "I thought he was just a witness."

Greene gave the homeless man a hard look. "He tried to run, after he told the patrolmen about what he found."

"Any possibility he dropped that package off himself?"

"Hell I did!" the guy said. "Told the cops what I found, then I tried to leave! This is still America, isn't it?"

Booth sized up the guy. "It's America, but you'll excuse me if I don't just take your word as gospel."

"Free country," the guy said with a shrug.

Greene said, "Two other people verified that someone else took the bag down the alley. They're with a forensic artist back at the precinct. Unfortunately, both got a better look at *this* guy than they did the delivery boy with the bag."

"That's just peachy," Booth said. To the homeless guy, he said, "What's your name?"

"Pete."

"Pete what?"

"I'm hungry."

"You won't get a meal till we're through here," Booth said.

The blue eyes sparked. "I'm gettin' a meal outa this?"

"Maybe. What's your last name?"

"These cuffs hurt, too, y'know. Can't eat with cuffs on."

Booth let out an irritated sigh.

Brennan intervened. "Lieutenant, will you remove the cuffs, please?"

"If I do, he's just going to try to run again."

"Probably," Pete admitted, bobbing his shaggy head.

Pointing to a restaurant two doors up the street, Brennan said, "You really want dinner?"

"Is the Pope Catholic?"

"If I get your cuffs taken off, can you eat and talk at the same time? And by talk, I mean answer our questions?"

The homeless man considered that. "Could I have a beer?"

Brennan held up an index finger in the man's face. "One beer, one dinner—you answer our questions."

"No cuffs?"

"No cuffs."

"How about another beer after dinner?"

"If you've been straight with us, sure."

A smile blossomed in the bush of Pete's beard. "Done deal!"

Pete turned his back to Greene so the lieutenant could undo the bracelets.

"This may be a bad idea," Greene said, but he did it anyway.

"If he runs, you could shoot him," Brennan suggested.

Pete's head jerked.

Brennan could tell Pete wanted to think she was

kidding, but she made sure her face gave away nothing.

The restaurant was a Mexican joint and they took a booth near the back—or anyway, that was where the hostess sat this oddly mixed group.

With Booth and Brennan on one side, Greene was forced to sit next to aromatic Pete. The crowd was thin, the salsa spicy, the beer cold.

When they were each nursing a Tecate, Booth asked, "So, Pete—what did you see?"

Pete didn't have his large combination plate yet, but he munched chips and salsa, sipped his beer, and nodded at Booth's question. "I was across the street, headed for my alley."

"*Your* alley," Booth said. "That's the one next to the Biograph?"

"Naw. I got a place a couple of blocks down . . . but I was headed that way when I saw the guy get out of the car."

Booth leaned forward. "Did you see the car?"

"Sure did."

"Did you see what *kind*?"

"Oh yeah. You bet."

"*What* kind, Pete?

"Blue."

Brennan felt Booth tense next to her and she spent the next several seconds concentrating very hard on the label of her beer.

With the expression of a nearsighted person trying

unsuccessfully to thread a needle, Booth asked, "You, uh, wouldn't know the make of car?"

Pete shook his head. "Last car *I* owned was a 1968 Dodge. Somehow, I haven't kept up."

Booth nodded his surrender. "And you didn't get the plate number."

It was a statement, not a question.

"Nope." Pete took a deeper drink from his beer. "He was weird, this guy. Which is why I noticed him."

When somebody like Pete found somebody else "weird," that was worth a listen.

"Weird how?" Booth asked, perking up.

"Dressed like crap, this guy."

"Define 'dressed like crap.' "

Pete thought for a second, munched a chip. "Dressed like me—dirty face like me, too . . . only he got out of a big new-lookin' car. That's weird to me. Isn't that weird to you?"

"Oh yeah," Booth said. "Was that on *this* block?"

"No . . . more like—east of Halsted over on Orchard . . . in front of some of them row houses? Guy parked in that residential neighborhood, probably 'cause nobody was around. He was lucky."

"Lucky?"

"Findin' a parkin' spot. Anyway, I was just cuttin' through, on my way back to my alley, like I said . . . and this guy gets out of the car lookin' homeless as hell, then he opens the trunk and yanks out this

garbage bag. He tosses it over his shoulder like fuckin'
Santa, and off he goes."

"Which way?"

"To the corner, then west on Fullerton to Lincoln,
and up to the alley. And me? I followed him the whole
way."

"*Why* did you follow him?"

"Are you kiddin'?" Pete snorted, and chewed a chip.
"He had a trash bag! ... *And* a nice car. If he was
dumping something that he had to take blocks from
the car, that meant he didn't want nobody to find it.
And if he didn't want nobody to find it, maybe he *was*
Santa, and Christmas come early for Pete this year."

Brennan looked at Pete in a new light. He definitely
wasn't homeless because he was a mental case.

Gently she asked, "Pete, why is a smart fella like
you on the street?"

Pete shrugged. "Havin' lots of stuff never brought
me anything but pain—I decided to cut my losses and
carry a lighter load."

She wasn't sure she knew what he meant, and she
was about to ask something else when Booth cut in.

"What did 'Santa' look like?"

"I told ya! A homeless-lookin' dude!"

"Be specific, Pete. Sing for your supper."

Pete thought and chewed another chip; salsa dotted
his beard now. "Shorter than me, stooped over a little,
like he was old ... but not so much right away, he sort

of got that way as he carried the bag. Like maybe it was gettin' to him? Dude wore sunglasses, too—like a homeless guy could afford expensive sunglasses!"

Booth tilted his head. "How do you know they were expensive sunglasses?"

"I dunno. Just looked like it to me. I mean, the ones that get thrown out that I can salvage are usually cheapies that got left behind or expensive ones that got busted."

"You didn't get a good look at his face?"

"Just that he had it all smeared with dirt. He was white, if that's where you're goin'."

"Any distinguishing marks? Anything at all?"

Pete shook his head and finished his beer, milking every drop.

Then he posed a question to Brennan: "You sure I can't have that other beer now? I mean, I been talkin' like crazy for you people, and it'll go swell with my meal."

"Sure," Brennan said.

Booth accepted this, and waved the waitress over and ordered Pete's second Tecate.

Then the FBI man asked Lieutenant Greene, "Can you get someone over to run the scene on Orchard?"

"After we finish eating," Greene said, "I'll take Pete over there, and he can show me where the guy parked the car."

"I'll do that," Pete said, bargaining some more, "if you promise me a ride back to my alley."

Greene nodded, and even smiled a little.

"You guys are the nicest cops I run into in a long time," Pete said. To Brennan he said, "And you're the foxiest."

Booth grinned and so did Brennan, flushing a little, saying, "Thanks, Pete."

Their food arrived and they mostly ate in silence—if Pete's enthusiastic style of putting food away could accurately be described as silent. . . .

When the meal was winding down, Brennan turned to Booth. "What do you make of the note?"

Booth glanced at Pete, whose full attention was devoted to his large combination plate. Like Brennan, the FBI agent clearly didn't consider talking in front of Pete much of a risk.

"Two different signatures?" he asked. "The 'clock' is running? Male victims in the neighborhood? I think the note writer is just screwing with us, typing anything that comes into his head."

"A few gay bars in the neighborhood," Greene pointed out.

"That's just it," Booth said, warming to the topic. "He'll get us to go off on some wild-goose chase while he laughs his ass off at us."

Greene thought for a moment. "Like he's been laughing at us cops, you mean?"

"I didn't say that."

"You didn't have to—the bastard's note did. He's supposedly been active for how long?"

Brennan said, "One of the bones might be as much as forty years old . . . but we don't know for sure yet."

Greene scowled, waved that off. "Forty years and we didn't tip to him? And catch him? That's bull-shit."

"One thing *isn't* bullshit," Booth said. "This guy's got access to skeletons, and some of them are old. We find out where he's getting them, maybe we find him."

Greene sighed. "We'll do what we can."

After Booth paid the check, they went outside into the cool, clear night.

Greene and Pete headed for the cop's car, and Booth—who had found a place to park his Crown Vic before they went to dinner—headed off in the oppo-site direction, Brennan hustling to keep up.

"Hey!" she yelled. "Where's the fire?"

He stopped and smiled. "Just walking off din-ner . . . and some frustration."

They continued up the well-lit street.

As they walked north on Lincoln Avenue, Chicago blues poured out of several bars, dance music out of others; and a few of the shops still had their lights on. They passed a club called Centre Stage, which, accord-ing to the marquee, tonight featured entertainment by a group of cross-dressing singers called Cher and the Cher-alikes.

"He could be stalking gay men, at that," Brennan said, but not pushing it.

Booth gave a one-shouldered shrug. "He wouldn't be the first . . . but forty years? Only way he could not've got on the local PD's radar is if he struck only very, very occasionally over all those years."

"I suppose."

"Greene's probably right—that's a long time to go without getting noticed, much less caught."

"Depends on his victims, though, doesn't it?"

He stopped and turned to her. "Meaning?"

She stopped, too. "Meaning that if his victims are very young men and older men, you don't really have a neat cross section of missing persons. And if he's hunting in a segment of the population that doesn't always get full service from law enforcement—"

"Hey, I treat everybody equally."

"That's probably true of most law enforcement these days," she agreed, "but think how homophobic the Chicago police would've been when this character started out."

He did think about that, then started walking again, quickly.

Catching up, she said, "Even now, gay people at least *feel* like they never get a fair shake from law enforcement."

Though he was less than happy, Booth said, "Granted."

"How accurate do you suppose missing persons records are, really?"

He didn't respond.

"Pete goes missing, for instance—who would ever know?"

Booth continued to walk in silence.

"What about young boys running away?"

Nothing.

"Face it, Booth, if this guy's smart . . . and his reconstruction of those remains tells me he is . . . my question isn't why hasn't he been caught by now—it's how do you *ever* expect to catch him?"

He stopped and faced her again. "Simple."

"Yeah? How, then?"

He twitched a smile. "Why—with your help."

They walked on.

5

SEELEY BOOTH COULD HARDLY BELIEVE HOW
pleasant walking with Brennan seemed.

She'd annoyed him with her generalization about
law enforcement treating gays unfairly; but she'd clarified that well enough.

And now he felt he'd just been too touchy about
the subject. Hell, he'd been too touchy about everything lately. . . .

Now, with her here, at his side, the two of them
strolling along anonymously on this big city street,
the evening cool, the nightlife just starting to hop, he
felt . . . fine.

"What's bothering you?" she asked.

Wasn't that wonderful—here he was, feeling great,
and she thought he looked like something was bothering him.

"Nothing." He glanced sideways at her. "What makes you think something's bothering me?"

She chuckled, which was a warm, surprising sound: he didn't think he'd ever heard her laugh before, at least not in that way.

He found himself smiling a little, and asked, "Oh, so now you're *laughing* at me?"

Smiling a little herself, she said, "I seem to be."

"Why?"

"It's just that . . . that's such a universal male response." She lowered her voice and aped his reaction. "Nothin'."

He did not respond, instead working at ignoring the tickle at the corners of his mouth.

She shook her head, but the smile remained. "Why is it so hard for men to admit something is wrong? Why so defensive?"

"I was not defensive."

"Well—you were brooding, then."

"I was not brooding! Anyway, men are wired to fix what's wrong, not bitch about it."

"Talking isn't 'bitching,' " Brennan said, the smile a bit condescending now.

". . . Hey, I didn't mean 'bitch' in any kinda, you know, way that'd—"

"Get you in trouble."

Booth nodded, then shrugged. "If I really talked about what's on my mind, *you'd* call it bitching."

"Hey. Go ahead and bitch."

He waited till they got past a blues club, from which funky music emanated, then said, "I'm supposed to focus on this Skel deal, but my head is still on that damn Musetti."

Her forehead creased sympathetically. "He's part of an important case—*your* case."

"Right, and I was responsible for his safety. Musetti may not be part of either of our skeletons, but he's almost surely dead. Snatched out from under—"

"You weren't even there," Brennan said.

"Right! Right. And maybe I should have been."

". . . How's it working out for you?"

"How's what working out for me?"

"This whole . . . omniscience thing. Where you're Superman?"

He stopped and grinned at her. "Was that a joke, Bones? I didn't think you did jokes. And a pop cultural reference yet!"

He couldn't tell whether it was a smile or a frown she was suppressing as she said, "I don't spend *all* my time in the lab."

He just stared at her, raising one eyebrow.

Her chin crinkled in near laughter; so it *had* been a smile, after all. . . .

"All right," she admitted. "I didn't *used* to spend all my time in the lab. I had a childhood, for instance. An actual life. I do know *some* things."

He began to walk again and she fell in at his side.

"I wasn't brooding—if you don't mind me saying, I

was finding it kind of pleasant, walking along, not arguing with you."

Another chuckle. "Well, that didn't last long."

"You're not all wrong, though—I *am* frustrated, having to spend all my time on this Skel serial deal. . . . No offense . . ."

Brennan said, "None taken."

". . . and after months on that one case? Right now I feel like the Gianellis are slipping through my damn fingers and there's not a frickin' thing I can do to stop it."

She said, "You have my permission to say 'fucking' in front of me, Booth. I won't wither and die like a frail, fragile flower."

That got a genuine laugh out of him. "You know, Bones—you're just the right medicine for me tonight. You up for a Starbucks?"

She was.

After they somehow negotiated their way into two no-nonsense black coffees—which seemed to confuse the barista, who'd apparently never filled such an outlandish order—they sat in the cafe's plush chairs and talked some more.

She said, "I certainly get why this Musetti matter is still on your mind. Where were you on the investigation, when our serial killer so rudely interrupted?"

He shook his head. "Nowhere with the Gianellis, really—several of us interviewed them, but they're not giving up word one."

Her clear blue eyes were thoughtful yet alert. "What about the agents you said were guarding Musetti?"

"We went over everything with them—sounds from when they were traveling, voices they might have heard, smells, everything. Bupkus."

"What other avenues are there?"

Booth sipped his coffee. "Still haven't found the escape vehicle."

"Prints at that house, where your witness was grabbed?"

"None . . . none but those of the guys guarding him and Musetti himself, anyway."

She said nothing.

Booth grunted a sort of laugh. "A print woulda been a miracle at *that* crime scene. Hell, there was no evidence at all—like *ghosts* grabbed him."

She frowned. "You don't have any other ways to track your witness down? I mean, it's not my field, forgive my ignorance; but you FBI agents do have resources."

Booth shook his head again. "We're working on it, but things are moving slowly. We talked to Musetti's girlfriend three or four times."

"There's a girlfriend?"

"Lisa Vitto. Works at a restaurant called Siracusa in Oak Brook. Owned by the Gianellis, by the way."

"Not real conducive for getting her to talk, huh?"

"Not really. But we didn't talk to her at the restaurant—we're not entirely stupid. We did our questioning at her apartment. Still, nada."

"Did you try a female agent?"

Booth's brow knit. "No—you really think that'd make a difference? That's a little sexist, coming from you, Bones."

"Not sexist, or reverse sexist, either. Realist." She sat back in her chair. "Some women are just more comfortable talking to other women."

He waved that off. "Maybe, but I don't think Ms. Vitto knows anything, anyway. She didn't know where Musetti's safe house was, so she couldn't have set him up, unintentionally or otherwise."

"Are you sure Musetti didn't tell her?"

"Nothing's certain in this world, but the guy was under our thumb, 24/7."

She arched an eyebrow. "Well, he was till they snatched him."

"That was cold, Bones—but accurate. Still, it would've been tough for Musetti to set this up himself to disappear . . . and, if he did, Ms. Vitto hasn't gone to meet him yet. . . . Nah, there's no way she could know anything. We're just fishing."

"I have a suggestion."

"Why am I not surprised?"

"If we concentrate on the case at hand, we can get you back on that mob inquiry, sooner than later."

Booth didn't want to hear this, but he knew Brennan was right.

One thing at a time.

Finish the Skel case, then back to Musetti. Other agents were taking up his slack on that investigation, anyway—and he'd been getting daily written reports.

Amounting to zip.

They eventually exited the Starbucks and meandered back to the car, then drove to the nearest twenty-four-hour Kinko's/FedEx, and sent the first skeleton's worth of bones to the Jeffersonian.

At night, the hallways of the Jeffersonian Museum could seem spooky to Angela Montenegro.

Tall, with curly dark hair falling to her shoulders, Angela—a scientist with the Jeffersonian's anthropology department—had the heart of an artist.

The work here with Dr. Temperance Brennan and the rest creeped her out at times, and more than once she'd considered tendering her resignation.

But in the end, her loyalty to Brennan won out.

Tonight, Angela—in dark slacks and a short-sleeved black blouse beneath her blue lab coat—walked the corridor toward the lab with soft drink in one hand, package of Twinkies in the other, not noticing anything even remotely spooky.

The rest of the team was in the lab—except for their fearless leader, of course, who was in Chicago with Booth and doing God only knew what. That thought caused a sneaky smile to cross her lips and she dismissed it just as quickly.

Actually, with the workload getting heavier by the day, Angela was wishing her best friend was at her side and not in the Windy City.

She opened the door into the lab and stood for a second, taking in the familiar but impressive surroundings. Unlike the staid, academic quality of the rest of the museum, the lab had an otherworldly air.

The Medico-Legal Laboratory—which had the ability to seal itself in airtight Plexiglas in case of a biohazard emergency—gave off a science-fiction vibe with its stainless-steel framing, Plexiglas backlit worktables, and translucent storage units consuming several walls.

On the other hand, the higher you looked, the more the place seemed like an old-time European railroad station; she'd seen a number of these on trips to the continent with her musician father.

The open-beamed ceiling consisted of translucent panels letting in light by day and giving the sensation of the beams melting into the dark sky at night. Somehow, that made the chamber appear even brighter under its harsh fluorescent lighting.

Brennan's assistant, the oh-so-young Zach Addy, leaned over a table to her left, bones laid out in their basic anatomic position, the chalky array maintaining a hypnotic hold on his bespectacled eyes. To her right, gaze glued to a microscope, curly-haired Jack Hodgins studied some bug or other.

They were a disparate bunch, thrown together in this lab by their gathered talents and fate, each with his or her own set of foibles, habits, and annoyances (both given and taken).

Brennan, their queen bee, hovered over the hive and, despite her occasional lack of social graces, the anthropologist had somehow overseen their growth from hodgepodge of "squints," as Booth called them, to the family they now were.

On her belt, her cell phone chirped. She jammed the Twinkies into the pocket of her lab coat, hiding the evidence.

The cell rang again and both Zach and Hodgins's heads popped up, frowning at the interruption, each looking around like a prairie dog sensing imminent danger.

Snatching the phone off her belt, Angela answered on the third ring.

"It's me," Brennan said, sounding tired.

"What's up, sweetie?" Angela asked right away. "You and Booth up to no good?"

"No, this is something else."

Angela grinned. "Should I ask? Is it dirty?"

". . . When I get back, you and I need to talk."

"What?" Angela asked, almost offended. "I can't be concerned about your social life? What kind of friend would I be if I ignored—"

"A great friend," Brennan said cheerfully, then pushed on: "I've sent you a package at the museum. I need you, Zach, and Jack to run all the tests you can, and tell me everything there is to know about what's inside."

"What *is* inside?"

"An entire skeleton . . . only it's not just one body."

"I know it's your line, honey, but—I don't know what that means."

"It means there's enough bones to make a skeleton, but multiple bodies provided them. Somebody assembled a sort of . . . fake skeleton, real though the individual parts may be."

"Parts is parts, huh?"

"I don't know what *that* means, Angela."

"Are you making fun of me, sweetie?"

"Possibly—but for sure I need you to identify how many people comprise this one skeleton; and, if possible, ID them."

"Oh, is *that* all?"

"And I need it an hour ago."

Angela glanced toward Zach and Hodgins.

They must have realized she was talking to Brennan and now were moving slowly toward her, friendly stalkers.

Into the phone she said, "You *are* making fun of me . . . and the sick part is, you're even starting to sound like Booth. Y'know, I'm not sure you two should be spending so much time together."

"Well, you can think about that till my package arrives; then get right on it."

"You know we will, sweetie." Angela closed her phone.

"We will . . . what?" Hodgins asked, suspicious.

Hodgins thought everything from the government to television to his breakfast cereal was part of some conspiracy or other to keep the regular people from finding out the truth—whatever that might be.

Generally, Angela considered her colleague just a little off center; but when his conspiracy theories sounded especially plausible, as they sometimes did, he scared her a little.

"We're going to test the skeleton that Temperance is FedExing to us."

"Hmm," Hodgins said, skepticism in his voice but the hint of a smile at a corner of his mouth. He did love his work. "That's it?" he asked.

"We do that all the time," Zach piped in, in a *no biggie* manner.

"This one's a little different," she said, popping the top on her soda.

"Different?" they asked together. "How?"

"One skeleton," she said. "Multiple donors. . . ."

Booth parked the Crown Vic under the hotel's portico. He got the door for Brennan, then helped her get her bag out of the trunk.

"Are you coming to the museum with me tomorrow?" Brennan asked him.

He nodded. "That's the plan."

"Pick me up early. I want to be there first thing."

"You got it, Boss."

". . . Booth, that wasn't an order."

"Kinda sounded like one."

She tried again: "Pick me up early, please."

"No problem," he said, and offered a smile.

She gave him a crooked smile in return, then grabbed her bag and rolled it through the revolving door into the lobby.

Booth turned the key in the ignition and, without even thinking about it, turned the Crown Vic toward the office.

End of the day was his only chance to check up on the Musetti/Gianelli case.

The next morning, Booth was (as requested) early.

Brennan waited inside the lobby until he pulled up, then walked out and got into the car.

She wore a brown blouse with tan slacks and a clunky wooden necklace, with a brown velvet jacket to keep off the autumn chill.

When she had her seat belt on, he handed her a coffee in a paper cup with a plastic lid—as established at Starbucks last night, hot and black.

"Did you have breakfast?" he asked.

She shook her head.

He pointed to a paper bag on the floor of the passenger side.

Brennan picked it up and opened it. "Bagels—perfect."

He drove, she ate, and little conversation ensued on their half-hour journey—Booth felt awkward, for some strange reason. Last night had been friendly, but this new day would require a professional tone that he (and for that matter she) didn't feel like establishing.

Once again, Dr. Jane Wu was waiting for them in the Field Museum lobby, but this time Lieutenant Greene was there, too, holding a box marked POLICE EVIDENCE.

As he and Brennan approached, the doctor and the cop did not at first notice the visitors, caught up in their own conversation.

Greene was saying, "How can you be a football fan in Chicago and *not* be a Bears fan!"

Dr. Wu grimaced. "I went to school in Boston. Patriots rule. Bears lose."

Shaking his head, Greene said, "Kicked your butt in '85, though."

"Ancient history. Who won three of the last four Super Bowls?"

Greene had no answer for that.

Brennan whispered to Booth, "Looks like you've been replaced."

Booth whispered back, "Well, you don't have to sound so pleased about it. . . ."

Dr. Wu waved. "Morning, you two! I've got the room all ready."

Booth and Brennan exchanged greetings with Lieutenant Greene, while Dr. Wu pointed out redundantly, "The lieutenant here was nice enough to bring the evidence, so we're good to go."

Brennan nodded. "Let's get at it, then."

The tables in the basement chamber were empty now, and Dr. Wu had Lt. Greene place the box on the one farthest from the door, after which she and Brennan would work at the middle station.

While the two doctors began, Booth and Greene found a coffee machine in a break room down the hall. The FBI agent bought, and the two men sat down at a small round table.

The room was empty this early in the day and neither man seemed to mind the quiet. Booth nursed the coffee—already his second of the day—not wanting to blast off on a caffeine high.

Booth asked the Chicago detective, "Did you get anything else from our homeless witness? Pete?"

Greene shook his head. "No. But I gotta say, ol' Pete was pretty cool, as homeless guys go. Led me to the parking place used by our skeleton transporter."

"Your crime scene unit get anything?"

Greene grunted a frustrated laugh. "Nothing."

"What about the neighborhood?"

"Got a team checking that."

"Cold cases in that part of town?"

Greene sipped his coffee. "My partner's checking

missing persons cases going back forty years. Your people find anything?"

"Nothing yet. But my partner, Woolfolk, is on it."

"I thought the girl was your partner."

Booth's eyebrows hiked. "Don't let her hear you calling her a 'girl,' Lieutenant Greene ... but she's sort of my partner on this, too—on the skeleton side of it, anyway."

Greene tilted his head. "Something you should know—I've got a call into a guy I know ... about a possible suspect."

"A suspect?"

"Don't get fired up. This is from years ago."

"So's part of our first skel. Hey, I don't care if it's from a hundred years ago—spill."

Greene sighed and looked down at his coffee. "It was in that neighborhood. Guy lived on that same street—Orchard, I mean. This was, oh, twenty years ago easy. . . . I was a fresh-faced kid hardly out of the academy. Detectives were working some missing person cases ... gay guys—several had gone missing from that neighborhood."

Booth twitched with irritation. "And you didn't say anything last night?"

Greene patted the air with one palm. "I'm getting to it, I'm getting to it. . . . Anyway, our guys had no real evidence, but there was this one suspect who looked good for it. Looked good to me, I mean—but who was I? Just a wet-behind-the-ears recruit fresh out of the academy."

"Nobody else went for your theory?"

"Not really. . . . The suspect in question . . . a guy named Bill Jorgensen . . . was fifty then. These kids, the young men, the victims, they were all in good health, some even worked out, and none of the guys at the precinct would take my ideas seriously. Just couldn't get them to believe that this fifty-year-old cat could take down strapping youths like these M.I.A. gays. Plus, back then even more than now, gay men were on the move—not transient exactly, but it was no shock if a gay man picked up and left. 'Cause of problems at work, say, or just the desire for fresh pastures. Lots of reasons."

Booth nodded. "Sure. But get to why you thought this older guy could've taken down young dudes."

Greene crumpled his coffee cup and made a good shot at a trash can half-a-room away. Then he turned to Booth with a steady gaze.

"This guy Jorgensen was in real good shape, especially for a guy of fifty. He hung out at gyms—he even worked at a few. Real physical fitness type."

"Makes sense. Anything else?"

Greene shook his head. "No real dead solid evidence against the guy . . . but he didn't have an alibi for the times a couple of the guys disappeared, plus he'd been seen in the bars where they disappeared from . . . though no one could put him *with* any of the guys."

"I see."

Greene shrugged. "Lot of circumstantial stuff, but nothing solid, and not enough to get a warrant. And as a newbie on the force, I could only push so hard."

Booth considered that for a long moment. "You didn't bring it up last night—why?"

"Two reasons. First, I hounded the guy so bad the first time, he got a restraining order against me. . . . Don't look at me like that, Booth—I was a kid, enthusiastic, and I thought I smelled a serial killer."

"Okay. I can understand that."

"Yeah, well understand this—I got a write-up in my file, and almost got canned. See, I spouted off to the media, and Jorgensen damn near sued the city over it. . . ."

"You said two things."

"Right. Second thing was, Jorgensen moved out of the neighborhood, and I lost track of him. Hell, he'd be seventy now, at least—I don't even know if the geezer's still alive."

"You could check up on him," Booth said.

Greene shook his head. "I am, but I'm using a snitch I trust—better to do it outside the system, first step, anyway. Even after all these years, too many people would shit bricks, me sniffing around Jorgensen again."

"Even if the feds did it?"

Greene raised both hands. "My boss, and his bosses, know we're in this together, Booth—and it wouldn't take Dick Tracy to figure out where you got the tip. Even those schmuck detectives who blew the case twenty years ago could figure *that* one out."

Booth sipped the last of his coffee, mulling all this.

Then he said, "This might be a pretty big leap to be taking."

Greene grunted another laugh. "Well, why don't we go after *your* suspect?"

Booth blinked. "What suspect?"

"Exactly," Greene said with a grin. "Give me a better idea, buddy, and I'll sign on with you."

Booth mulled it some more. "Well . . . it wouldn't hurt to look at this Jorgensen."

"Like I said, I've got a guy I should hear from sometime today." The cop took in a deep breath, held it, then finally blew it out. "You think we've got a chance in hell of catching this guy? If it is Jorgensen, he hardly even got on the radar, back in the day . . . and the only one who got in trouble was yours truly."

Booth studied the detective. "This isn't twenty years ago—you're an old pro . . . and I'm damn good, too."

"Plus, there's that 'girl' of yours," Greene said impishly. Or as impishly as a Chicago cop could say anything.

Booth said, "That 'girl' is a kind of genius, yeah, and in fact we've got good people all over this case—the best equipment, the best support, the best period."

They sat in silence for a moment, each drinking his coffee, lost in his own thoughts.

Greene said, "And yet this prick literally dumps his victim on your doorstep."

Booth nodded. "And the second one came pretty close to your doorstep—your turf, anyway."

The detective's upper lip curled. "If this is Jorgensen . . . the bastard's blowin' a Bronx cheer at both of us."

"Well, then—we'll just have to show him how foolish that was."

Booth and Greene stood around for most of the next four hours, alternately drinking coffee and talking football, both men periodically checking in by cell phone with colleagues on the case.

Finally, Brennan called them over to the table where she and Dr. Wu had laid out all the bones from the bag.

"Two hundred six bones," Brennan said. "Another complete skeleton."

"One person this time?" Booth asked.

"Not hardly," she said. "Our do-it-yourselfer is at it again. The femora?"

"The two big bones in the thighs," Booth said, glancing at Greene.

Brennan asked the FBI agent, "Notice anything different about them?"

Booth's eyes immediately went to the epiphyseal lines, which were both completely fused.

"No," Booth admitted.

Greene said, "One's longer than the other."

Seeing that now, too, Booth felt a twinge in his gut.

He was not about to let himself be drawn into a pissing contest with his new colleague—showing off for these two attractive women in this case. That kind of junior high nonsense had no place here, and, anyway, he and Greene would just wind up looking like testosterone-addled fools with these women, both of whom had more education than he and Greene put together.

Focus on the case, he told himself.

When his eyes rose to Brennan's, she was watching him; and Booth had the most unsettling feeling she could read his thoughts. . . .

"Both men had reached full adulthood," she was saying, "but one was ten centimeters shorter than the other."

"Ten centimeters," Booth mused.

Greene piped in with, "Four inches."

Not rising to the bait, Booth asked, "Meaning?"

Brennan gestured with an open palm. "Meaning, with this difference in femur length? Either the man was seriously deformed, or we're dealing with more than one body again."

Greene, interested, asked, "When you say 'man,' do you mean . . . man?"

"The brow ridges on the skull indicate a male, yes," Dr. Wu said. "More prominent than in females."

Brennan added, "The pelvic bones are male as well."

Nodding, Booth asked, "Anything else?"

"The fingers," Brennan said.

Booth looked down at the skeleton's hands.

The fingers were of differing lengths, which of course was normal; but, in this case, in an unnatural way—the left index finger longer than both the middle and ring fingers, one thumb long, one short, and another fingertip did not look quite right to Booth.

He asked, "Are you sure you've got the bones in the right places?"

Immediately he wished he hadn't said that, but he had said it, and earned Brennan's withering gaze.

He muttered, "Just asking."

"We do indeed have the bones in the *right* places," Brennan said.

Greene asked, "Walk us laymen through, would you?"

"Glad to," Brennan said. "The fingers are made up of several bones."

She pointed to each one as she ran down the list.

"There are the metacarpals," she continued, "the proximal phalanges, the middle phalanges, and the distal phalanges."

She held up her own hand.

"This is what a hand should look like, more or less . . . and as you can see, these two hands not only don't match each other, the fingers of each hand line up incorrectly."

Both Booth and Greene nodded in understanding.

Brennan went on: "Your suspect has used at least two bodies . . . and my guess is more . . . to build this specimen."

"Jesus Jones," Greene said.

"Same is true of the feet," Dr. Wu said, and she too gestured as she went. "Although all the bones are here, they obviously don't belong to just two feet. The wear and tear on them is all wrong."

Booth asked, "What about the end of this ring finger?" He pointed to the finger that had struck him odd.

"Broken," Brennan said. "A long time ago. That's one of the reasons we know that this finger came from at least two fingers—the distal phalange is practically smashed, while the middle phalange is perfectly normal."

"Why?" Booth asked. "Is that impossible?"

"No," she said, "but it's extremely rare . . . especially considering the extreme damage to the distal."

Brennan turned to Dr. Wu. "These two bones came from two different people."

Dr. Wu indicated her agreement.

"So," Booth said, "can we tell if any of these parts belong to any of the bones from the first skeleton?"

"Yes," Brennan said, "but not without more testing—I'll know more when I get it back to the Jeffersonian."

"You want to go with it?"

"Yes. This facility is fine, and I appreciate Dr. Wu's help and hospitality, but I can do a much—"

"Can't let you go, Bones," Booth cut in, shaking his head. "We've got two skeletons in two days—do you really think our madman's going to stop?"

Brennan's brow creased, and she thought for several long moments, but she didn't argue. "Then we'll package this one up and get it to the Jeffersonian ASAP."

"Good," Booth said. "What about the first skel?"

"I haven't checked in at the Jeffersonian this morning yet."

Brennan got her cell phone out of her purse and hit speed dial.

Angela picked up on the second ring, and Booth's sniper-sensitive hearing picked up her side of the conversation: "Sweetie, what's up?"

"Getting ready to send you a second skeleton."

"You've been busy. Where are you, Chicago or Sarajevo?"

"Still Chicago."

"This another reassembly job?"

"It is—I already detect at least two sources for the bones. Did you get the first skeleton yet?"

"First thing this morning—we've started DNA testing, and Jack is working on soil still attached to the bones."

"Excellent—don't be shy about calling when you have anything."

"These are not fast tests."

"*Somebody's* fast," Brennan said, "delivering two homemade skeletons in two days."

She clicked off.

Greene said, "I've gotta make a call myself—be right back."

Greene headed quickly out, and Booth watched as Dr. Wu and Brennan packaged the bones for shipment in a box about the size of a small end table. The last thing Brennan did was use a marker to write the address of the Jeffersonian on the top.

By the time she finished, Greene was back, shaking his head.

"I don't believe it," he said, walking over to Booth. "And I don't know if this is a good thing, or a bad one. . . ."

"Your favorite suspect Jorgensen's still alive?"

Brennan had perked at the word "suspect," but she said nothing.

"Yeah," Greene said. "Moved to the 'burbs . . . but he's still around."

Booth grinned. "You want to pay him a visit?"

Greene considered that. "Been a long time—twenty years. You think my old pal'll remember me?"

"Take out a court order on somebody," Booth said, "you tend to remember 'em. Makes an impression."

"What court order?" Brennan piped in.

Booth ignored that and said to the cop, "Is it still in effect, that court order?"

Shaking his head, Greene said, "Naw—thing's long since lapsed."

"*What* court order?" Brennan repeated.

Booth waved her off. "Long shot. Not your concern."

"Long shot," Greene echoed.

Brennan looked increasingly agitated.

On the move, Booth said, "Lieutenant Greene and I are going to take a little drive."

Brennan stepped in front of the FBI agent, blocking his path. An eyebrow was up. "Not without me, you're not."

Greene started to say something, but Booth just laid a hand on his arm. The detective stopped and gave the FBI agent a curious look.

Booth asked, "You want to go see your pal Jorgensen while he's still breathing?"

"Yeah. Sure. Of course."

Booth smirked good-naturedly. "Then don't get started with Bones here, or we'll *all* look like what's in that FedEx box by the time we get out of here."

Brennan glared at the Chicago cop.

"Well," Greene said, with a sideways look at Booth, "you said it yourself—she *is* your partner. . . ."

Brennan's eyes shifted to Booth, defiance gone, mouth open, but no words coming out.

Turning to Dr. Wu, Booth said, "Could we impose on you for one more favor . . . ?"

She nodded, ahead of him. "I'll make sure the package goes out with the FedEx stuff today."

Booth gave her his best smile. "Thanks."

Greene took his car while Booth and Brennan followed in the Crown Vic. The ride from the Field Museum to the suburb of Algonquin took the better part of an hour.

Their conversation along the way mostly consisted of Booth filling her in on this old suspect of Greene's.

But at one point, Brennan asked, "You told Greene I was your partner?"

". . . Yeah, I did."

"I thought that guy Woodfield was your partner."

"It's Woolfolk, and he's my FBI-assigned partner. But this is *our* case, Bones."

". . . Glad you see it that way."

"Well, I do."

"But Booth?"

"Yes?"

"Stop calling me Bones."

But that last didn't have much energy in it.

Booth followed Greene as he left the expressway for a four-lane main drag, then a two-lane residential street, and they wove around until the Chicago detective pulled to a stop in front of one of three small houses on a quiet cul-de-sac.

Jorgensen's residence sat in the middle, vacant lots on either side between him and his neighbors—a Tudor two-story, tan with brown trim, a two-car garage to the left, a sidewalk from the driveway to the one-step front porch.

The house, of 1970s vintage, was nice enough, well maintained if not impressive.

What it did not look like was the home of a homicidal maniac who left skeletons for the FBI.

Then again, Booth and other agents he knew had worked on serial killer cases, and in no instance had the perp's house looked like the gloomy Gothic mansion on the hill in *Psycho*.

If anything, the homes in question looked like every other house on the block, in the neighborhood, as anonymous as their owners. And like their owners, it was what was inside them that was decidedly different. . . .

Booth and Brennan met Greene at the end of the driveway. Looking around the end of the garage, Booth could see a chain-link gate that led to a fenced-in backyard.

"What's the plan?" Booth asked.

Greene's grin had a nasty edge. "I thought I'd

knock at the front door and, if Mr. Jorgensen is good enough to answer, just say hello. Renew an old acquaintance."

"Works for me," Booth said.

"What should I do?" Brennan asked.

"Hang back," Booth said.

"This is a seventy-year-old man. . . . I can handle—"

"Don't," Greene cut in, "underestimate this 'seventy-year-old man.'"

Brennan frowned. "I realize—"

Greene cut her off again. "If he did what I *think* he did . . . he'll have no hesitation, taking a human life. Dr. Brennan, you ever heard of a serial killer that stopped on his own?"

"I'll 'hang back,'" she said. "But I do have one more question. . . ."

"Go on," Greene prompted.

"What did Mr. Jorgensen do for a living?"

"When I was looking at him in those disappearances," Greene said, "Mr. Jorgensen taught anatomy at Saint Sebastian University."

"Never heard of it," Booth said.

Brennan's forehead crinkled.

Greene said, "Small school on the North Side, mostly medicine."

Brennan asked, "Any connection between the missing men and the university?"

"Not directly to Jorgensen," Greene said. "There

was a connection between a student of his, however, and one missing man. Never anything we could tie to Jorgensen, though—guy is a near miss in all of this; always just on the periphery."

"I suggest we go up and say hello," Booth said to Greene, "before the neighbors call him to ask about the trio of strangers chatting outside."

They went up the driveway, Greene in the lead, Brennan (as instructed) bringing up the rear.

As they moved up the walk, Booth unsnapped the safety latch on his pistol. Their guy might be seventy, but—as Greene had so forcefully made the point—Jorgensen was a suspect in multiple homicides.

Passing the living room window as they followed the walk, Booth thought he saw the curtains move, but couldn't be sure.

Just as Greene reached the step, the front door swung open and a small, sturdy man stepped out, holding the screen door open with his left hand.

The man was on the short side, five-eight maybe, with dyed black hair and prominent crow's-feet around dark eyes. He had a nearly lipless mouth, short straight nose, and wore tennis shoes, jeans, and a red tee shirt, sporting the massive biceps of a much younger man.

If this was Jorgensen, the old boy looked in better shape than half the FBI agents Booth knew.

"Help you folks?" the old guy said in a strong baritone, his expression not unfriendly, but tinged with skepticism.

Greene reached into his jacket pocket for his badge. "Mr. Jorgensen—"

For a split second Booth saw something in Jorgensen's eyes, and knew they were in trouble.

"*You!*" Jorgensen bleated.

The gun appeared from nowhere and the first shot hit Greene full in the chest, driving him back into Booth as the FBI agent tried to draw his own weapon.

The impact sent them both to the ground as Jorgensen raised his pistol to take a second shot.

Booth didn't have time to call out and stop her.

Brennan simply leapt over the fallen pair and spun, her right foot connecting with the gun and driving it out of Jorgensen's hand, sending it spinning across the porch as the old man retreated into the house, his hand catching Brennan's sleeve . . .

. . . and dragging her inside with him!

Struggling, rolling a stunned Greene off him, Booth checked that the lieutenant didn't appear seriously injured, then bounced to his feet, gun in hand.

Throwing the screen door open, he rocketed into the living room.

The living room had been a tidy place, he assumed, before Brennan and Jorgensen had made their way through it, tipping over a lamp, breaking a glass coffee table, and scattering magazines all over the hardwood floor.

Booth heard heavy breathing to his left. He passed the sofa, rounded a corner, and found himself in a dining room with a table and six chairs, three upended.

The fight had moved into the kitchen, and Booth moved with it, jumping over a chair, his pistol up, entering the room, where he discovered Jorgensen, holding a large butcher knife over his head.

Booth would have taken him then, if Brennan hadn't been between him and the killer, her back to the agent.

"Mr. Jorgensen," she said, her voice calm despite the ragged breaths between words. "We just came to talk."

"I've got nothing to say to you," he snarled, eyes wild, "*or* that asshole cop!"

"Bones," Booth said, "take a step either way."

Without turning to look at him, Brennan snapped, "Booth, shut up! . . . No one else is getting shot today."

The FBI agent scanned the kitchen, looking for another way to get to his target. It was a wide, open room full of stainless steel appliances and dark, hard counters.

"Maybe not shot," Jorgensen said, his upper lip curling to reveal very white, very false teeth. "But how about *stabbed*?"

He lunged at Brennan, blade and teeth flashing, and she dropped to the linoleum.

Booth squeezed the trigger, but Brennan swept Jorgensen's feet out from under him, so that Booth's bullet struck the old man in the shoulder, the knife flying out of his hand, clunking against the refrigerator as Brennan delivered an elbow to the old man's temple, knocking him cold.

The knife, meanwhile, had dropped to the floor.

No one moved.

The aroma of cordite singed the air. Booth's ears were ringing from the shot, his eyes glued to the knife sticking out of the linoleum inches away from Brennan.

Then Brennan got up, screaming at him. "What, are you *trying* to kill me?"

Suddenly, Booth's hearing didn't seem so damaged, though he would just as soon it had not recovered so quickly.

"I *told* you not to shoot. What part of that didn't you understand? Booth, that knife . . ."

He holstered his weapon, grabbed her by the arms, firm but not rough. "I was scared, too."

She backed away from him, obviously uncomfortable. "I . . . I wasn't scared, just . . . sizing him up. I had him, I . . ."

"Bones, you're shouting," he said.

"I *know* I'm shouting. A big lummox shot at me!"

"Not *at* you, *near* you. Save the rest for later—gotta get back to Greene."

On cue, Greene wobbled into the kitchen doorway,

his jacket off, his shirt ripped open to reveal a Kevlar vest, the bullet still protruding over his heart.

He gave them a lopsided grin. "God *damn*, that hurt. . . ."

"You okay?" Booth asked.

Greene swayed. "I've been worse. Not much worse, but . . ."

Sirens called from the distance.

Greene gestured with a trembling thumb toward the sound. "Called for backup. Not that you needed any."

The Chicago cop nodded down at the old man, the blood turning the red shirt maroon.

"That evil old fucker dead?" he asked.

"No," Booth said. "Brennan just knocked him out. With an elbow."

Greene looked at Brennan with wide, respectful eyes. "Whoa. Are you shittin' me?"

Booth grinned at the anthropologist. "Bones has unexpected skills."

Greene loomed over the suspect, having a closer look. "Remind me not to mess with you, lady. Regular Rambo in a dress."

Brennan's brow furrowed. "I'm not wearing a dress, and, anyway, I don't know what that means."

Greene gaped at Booth.

"She doesn't get out much," the FBI agent said.

Grabbing a towel off the counter, Brennan dropped to one knee and pressed it against the man's wound.

Sizing up Greene, Booth said, "Maybe you ought to sit down for a minute, pal. You look a little pale."

Greene leaned against the kitchen counter. "No matter how heroic it looks in the movies? Getting shot sucks."

Sirens screamed outside. "Evidently, Mr. Jorgensen still holds a grudge," Booth said.

Brennan looked up from the bandage. "Or Lieutenant Greene was right, and he's got something to hide."

Booth, eyes narrowed, said, "I'm with you, Bones. . . . Once the EMTs get here, we'll have a look around."

6

TEMPERANCE BRENNAN, ARMS FOLDED, CHIN high, the picture of a professional woman, was trembling.

As she stood outside the nondescript house—policemen, crime scene analysts, and EMTs hustling in and out—she had finally succumbed to fear . . . or at least an unsettled sense that she could not shake.

She hadn't lied to Booth: she really hadn't been scared in that kitchen, all her focus had been on Jorgensen and that knife.

But when Booth's bullet whizzed past her and struck Jorgensen, the knife heading in her direction, her grip on her self-control had vanished.

Flimsy thing, control.

One second you had it, next you didn't. One minute you're at the Jeffersonian studying an arrowhead in the chest of an eight-hundred-year-old Native American, next you're in Algonquin, Illinois, stanching the wound of a seventy-year-old probable serial killer.

Nice thing about the lab, *she* had control—*she* was in charge.

Things occasionally went differently than expected, but the lab was strictly science, and the unexpected was part of that too.

Not that there wasn't pressure at the Jeffersonian—a bone broke in the lab, it was generally hundreds if not thousands of years old . . . in a world where value was determined by whether bones were whole or not. But when things went wrong there, no bullets flew, no knives hurtled in your direction.

More Chicago cops were arriving, and the FBI had a large contingent on hand as well; the neighbors, few that there were, had turned out to watch. SAC Dillon was off to one side, giving Booth the third degree about the shooting, while Lieutenant Greene was being treated by EMTs in the yard.

An ambulance had already carted Jorgensen away to a hospital. The wound was not life-threatening, but the bullet would have to be removed, and the old boy needed to be stitched up.

Jorgensen would remain under police watch, and—at the very least—charged with attempted murder for shooting Lieutenant Greene and attempted assault on

Brennan. If the Chicago and FBI CSIs found evidence of more crimes in the house, that list could grow.

Brennan—with no one yet questioning her, treating her, or for that matter bothering to ask if she was okay—stood off to one side, alone.

Which was fine; she figured now would be a good time to keep a low profile, and stay out of the way.

This plan seemed to be working nicely until her cell phone rang.

When she reached for it on her belt, the cell got caught and kept ringing. Heads slowly turned her way. She finally got the thing loose and punched the button.

"Brennan," she said.

"Hi, sweetie," came Angela's cheerful voice.

Turning her back on Dillon, Booth, and the others, Brennan filled Angela in on everything that had happened since they last spoke.

"Oh my God," Angela said. "Are you all right?"

"Yes," Brennan said.

It was only a small lie.

"I'm not talking just physically, honey, but mentally—emotionally. You must be—"

"I appreciate your concern, Ange, but where are you with the first skeleton?"

". . . Trying to identify the different components, but frankly, it's slow going."

Not what Brennan wanted to hear.

On the other end, she heard a small commotion, and Angela interrupted their conversation to talk to someone, then was back.

"Jack wants you," Angela said. "Hang on."

Dr. Jack Hodgins, the staff entomologist, knew more about spores and minerals than the science department of your average university.

"Temperance," he said, each syllable a machine-gun bullet. "How's Chicago? And by that I mean, did you solve the assassination of Anton Cermak yet?"

"I don't know what that means."

"Nineteen thirty-four, Capone gang CEO Frank Nitti had Mayor Cermak whacked in Miami. Press of the day made out it was a miss on FDR, but it was really a hit on His Honor."

Shaking her head, Brennan asked, "Interesting to know, but not terribly helpful. Got anything relevant for me, Jack?"

"C'mon, Doctor, you're in Chicago! It's like . . . the Disney World of conspiracies! Vote early, vote often, the Chicago Seven . . ."

"I meant relevant to the case," she interrupted.

"Oh," Jack said. "Well. Sorry. Yeah, I've got some preliminary findings about the soil still clinging to the bones."

She waited.

"The silica and oxygen content of the soil is *very* high."

"*Sand?*"

"Not sand like beachfront . . . but very sandy soil."

"In Chicago?"

"Yeah," Jack said. "That was my first reaction—get past the lakefront, what's sand got to do with the Second City, right? But then I got to thinking about just how big that lake really is."

"The bones were from bodies that were buried on the beach?"

"Say that fast, three times. . . . No, not in sand, sandy *soil*."

"Which means?"

"Which means this ground is probably around the lake somewhere, near but not actually *at* the lake . . . maybe by a river, or even out in the 'burbs. Plus, it's nutrient rich, so a marsh maybe. Not acidic enough to be from a bog."

"That takes in a lot of area," Brennan sighed. "Do you know where in greater Chicago that might be?"

"We're working on it. Got some other tests still ongoing—I'll tell you more when I know more."

"All right, Jack," she said.

After quick good-byes, she clicked off.

Brennan went looking for Booth, found him huddled on the driveway with Dillon and the Chicago PD crime scene crew.

They all parted and turned to look at her as she approached.

"What's the deal?" she asked, stopping in the gap they had made in their little circle.

Booth said, "This is Lieutenant Ron Garland."

A tall, thin man with a blond butch haircut and sad blue eyes stepped forward. He wore gray slacks, a white shirt open at the throat, and a navy windbreaker with the words CHICAGO POLICE CRIME SCENE UNIT emblazoned over the left breast.

"Ron, this is Dr. Temperance Brennan," Booth said, and Brennan shook hands with the man. "Tell her what you told me."

After clearing his throat, Garland said, "Uh, Ms. Brennan, it's an honor to meet you. . . . I, uh, just loved your book."

Brennan smiled and looked away—she always felt awkward meeting the public, though hearing praise from a law enforcement professional pleased her.

Still, she never knew what to say beyond "Thank you," which she did.

"Not that," Booth said, frowning at the crime scene lieutenant. "About the *house*."

Garland shot a glare at the FBI agent, as if about to tell the fed where to go.

Brennan interceded, saying, "Don't take offense— tact isn't Agent Booth's strong suit."

Garland responded to Brennan with a small smile, then quickly morphed back to dead serious. "Dr. Brennan, we found a hidey-hole in the bedroom closet . . . and came up with this."

Another investigator stepped forward and displayed a huge green album already sealed in a plastic evidence bag.

"What is it?" Brennan asked.

"A sort of keepsake book," Garland said. "A, uh . . . what you'd have to call a scrapbook."

Brennan's eyebrows climbed. "Really? What *sort* of scrapbook?"

"When I say scrapbook, I mean that literally," Garland said. "Sickest shit I've ever seen . . . and I've seen some."

Something slithered in Brennan's stomach. "How literally?"

Garland heaved a sigh that started in his toes and ended in his scalp. "He apparently peeled a piece of skin from each of his victims . . . and pressed it into his scrapbook."

She swallowed, the things slithering in her stomach seeming to multiply and fight for space.

Now Garland's eyebrows rose. "And I'm afraid that may not be the worst thing."

Brennan braced herself. "How could it *not* be?"

"There's a crawlspace."

Immediately, Brennan felt better.

"Actually," she said, "that's not worse."

Garland blinked.

"I'm sorry," she said. "I meant that only from a standpoint of investigating a crime scene. This kind of thing . . . well, it's my turf."

Garland relaxed, apparently knowing he didn't have to say anything more.

And he didn't: Brennan already knew what the crime scene lieutenant was talking about, and what he wanted. In an instant, all was clear: her squirmy stomach over the scrapbook, her posttraumatic anxiety about the fight in the kitchen, were gone.

For the first time since they had left the Field Museum this afternoon, she really felt like herself.

"Show me," she said to the lieutenant.

Brennan and Booth followed Garland through the living room, dining room, and into the kitchen.

Around the corner from the refrigerator, out of sight from the other doorway, was a door she had not noticed before. This led to a mudroom with a washer and dryer, beyond which was another door, now open to the two-car garage.

Garland stopped just before he got to the garage door and turned to face Booth and Brennan. He motioned for them to take a step back, which they both did—Brennan caught between Booth and the washer.

Garland pointed to the floor.

Brennan saw a hatch carved into it, a small metal ring set in an indented area on the side nearest her.

"Crawlspace," Garland said.

She traded a look with Booth, who seemed more unnerved about this than she did.

Which somehow felt reassuring. Big sniper guy, uneasy about a dark place in the floor. A place she would go without hesitation or fear, even already knowing what waited down there.

After snapping on a pair of latex gloves, Brennan crouched, grabbed the ring, and lifted, the door raising easily, a safety hinge latching when the lid was up all the way, holding it in place.

The smell, faint though it was, hit her instantly.

Looking up at Garland, she said, "You're right— something's decomposing under this house."

Neither man said anything as she eased forward, sat on the edge, and let her legs dangle into the dark crawlspace.

Garland handed her down a Mini MagLite and she screwed its head half a turn, providing a fairly wide beam.

She smiled up at the troubled men and said, "Fellas—it's going to be all right."

Then she dropped through the door into a crouch.

She found herself in a large area with a dirt floor and less than three feet of clearance to the joists of the house's main floor.

On her hands and knees, she moved forward, the beam of light sweeping back and forth. She tried to follow the smell of decay, which so permeated the space she did not wonder what awaited her; she knew: *death.*

The only question that remained at this point was . . . *how many?*

Finally making it to what (if she had her bearings

right) must be the front wall, she sent the beam into a corner, revealing a stack of bags of agricultural lime.

Some bags were full, most empty.

The house was not huge, but the crawlspace seemed to be open under all of it. Thinking of her two skeletons formed from different remains, she saw plenty of room down here for enough bodies to make several more.

She took a more circuitous route back to the door, skirting the far end of the house, and she was just about to turn back when the light caught something shiny.

Even when she got right above it, she could not see it clearly.

Then, brushing away some dirt, she saw what looked like a diamond ring.

She cleared away more earth, using her fingers, digging tiny bits at a time until she saw that the ring encircled a finger, the finger was attached to a hand, and the hand to an arm.

She went back to the hatch and looked up to see both Garland and Booth peering in.

To Garland she said, "I need work lights—enough to illuminate the whole area down here. And can you rig up some way to blow clean air in?"

The Crime Scene lieutenant nodded and grinned. "Lights and air conditioning, Dr. Brennan—no problem."

To Booth she said, "Call Dr. Wu. . . . No, wait, help me up out of here and I'll do it."

Garland and Booth both extended a hand. She took them both and let them pull her up out of the hole.

"Thanks, guys," she said.

The two men exchanged wan glances, apparently spooked a little by how nonchalant Brennan was in the presence of death.

Booth handed her his cell phone. "Jane's number's up—just hit the green button."

She nodded, surprised he didn't have Dr. Wu on speed dial yet.

The Field Museum anthropologist picked up on the first ring and Brennan explained the situation and what she needed.

"I could bring a couple of interns," Dr. Wu said.

"No room. They'll just end up cramped and bored. Better if it's just the two of us."

"Might take me a while to get there."

"No real rush," Brennan said. "The victims aren't going anywhere. Just make sure you've got every-thing. My gut tells me, when we do get started? We're going to be at this for some time."

Brennan ended the call. "Know where we can get a cadaver dog?" she asked Booth.

"Cadaver dog?"

"An animal that works like a bomb-sniffing dog, only it finds corpses."

Booth shook his head.

"In Chicago, neither do I," she said. "Let's get a tech with ground-penetrating radar instead."

Booth called in that request; while they waited for the tech and for Dr. Wu, Brennan and Booth tracked down Greene, in the front yard, smoking a cigarette.

"How you feelin', buddy?" Booth asked.

Greene managed a shrug. "By the time my boss got done reaming me out, my ass hurt more than my chest."

The FBI agent laughed. "Yeah, I got a rubber-glove exam, myself."

Brennan spoke up: "We captured a killer—a suspect who responded to our presence by shooting Lieutenant Greene, point blank. Since when does *that* rate a reprimand?"

Greene smirked but it was not at all nasty, merely weary. "The doc here really isn't law enforcement, is she?"

Booth didn't respond to Greene, but did answer Brennan: "Channels, Bones. Neither one of us went through channels."

"So what?"

"So, technically, the lieutenant and I aren't even working together. And taking along our resident anthropologist-slash-bone-expert, to confront such a dangerous suspect? Not exactly what either the FBI or the Chicago PD hand out merit citations for."

Brennan said, "Look, I put up with bureaucracy where I work—who doesn't? But this is absurd. . . ."

"Plus which," Greene put in, "I went and got myself shot. Bosses hate that—more paperwork. Shooting board. Union reps to deal with."

Brennan shook her head. "But the killer was captured!"

Booth said, "And that's the only reason why Greene and yours truly are not both hanging from a yardarm somewhere."

Turning to the FBI agent, Greene said, "Yeah, and I hate the yardarm."

Booth nodded. "So hard to get your shirts to fit right for a month after that."

"You're making jokes?" Brennan asked. "You get dressed down for catching a killer, and you make jokes about it?"

Booth shrugged. "I'm open to other options, should you have any."

She considered that, finally realizing nothing could be done about the vagaries of bureaucrats.

And yet she saw the system's side of it, too. Law enforcement couldn't just go around ringing every doorbell in America looking for bad guys.

Truth was they were lucky.

She only hoped their luck would hold out: chances were Jorgensen's attorney would try to turn this into some sort of harassment case and get all the evidence thrown out.

Brennan hadn't spent a lot of time in court, but she did understand that if you caught the wrong judge on the wrong day, your whole case could go out the window.

"I almost forgot," she said to the men. "I got a call from Jack right before I went into the crawlspace."

"Jack?" Greene asked.

"Dr. Jack Hodgins," Booth explained. "Member of Dr. Brennan's team at the Jeffersonian. . . . A squint."

Booth's favorite condescending jargon for scientific consultants like Brennan.

"Ah," Greene said with a nod, obviously familiar with the term.

Booth had the ability, perhaps unintentional, to bring out the little girl in Brennan, almost never in a good way: right now she wanted to kick him in the shins. Or higher.

Booth caught her glowering at him and said, all innocence, "What?"

Ignoring this typical insensitivity, Brennan said, "According to Jack, our first skeleton was buried in sandy soil."

Booth's eyes narrowed. "That's good to know, but *this* place surely doesn't have sandy soil. . . ."

"No it doesn't," she said.

Greene asked, "Are you sure about that, Doc?"

"Judging by what I was crawling around on, in that crawlspace? That dirt is clay."

Booth looked uneasy again. "What are you saying?"

"That our friend Mr. Jorgensen may indeed have constructed the skeletons . . . but if he did, they were not put together from bodies buried under this house."

Greene said, "Come on, Doc—I just know we're gonna find a shitload of skels under this place!"

Even Booth seemed jarred by the inelegance of the lieutenant's phrasing, but it was Brennan who said, coolly, "Be that as it may—it's highly doubtful our made-to-order 'skels,' as you put it, were composed of bones found under that crawlspace."

Booth was trying hard to salvage Jorgensen as their man. "But he could have another burial plot, right?"

"Sure," she agreed. "If he was striking at transients, and gay ones at that . . . the kind of people who, unfortunately, are able to fall off the planet without anyone much noticing, well . . . he could have been extremely ambitious, over all these years. And needed, and used, various sites."

Booth nodded crisply, then turned to Greene, asking, "What about Jorgensen's former residence?"

"We get the evidence here we're probably gonna get," Greene mused, "we could go back there and dig some more—but back in the day?"

By this Greene apparently meant during the first investigation of Jorgensen—the unsuccessful one that had led to a court order against the detective.

"Back then," Greene was saying, "we didn't find a goddamn thing."

Booth said, "Which means he may have had an off-site burial ground, and—"

Brennan interrupted, uncomfortable with how fast the FBI agent was moving. "Booth, he could have buried his victims in sandy soil anywhere within, I don't know, a hundred miles. It's useless to speculate. We'll work what we have here, and go from there."

Booth seemed about to retort, but thought better of it, putting a lid on; his eyes told her he knew she was right.

A tech arrived and conducted a sweep of the crawlspace with GPR, leaving behind yellow markers to indicate the probable location of bodies.

Dr. Wu and her tools arrived half an hour later.

She and Brennan donned coveralls, white paper masks covering both mouths and noses, and latex gloves; then they carted the tools into the laundry room and prepared to go down into the crawlspace.

The laundry room looked different now—extension cords running everywhere, a motor humming from a fan she could not see but knew must already be down in the crawlspace. Light leached up through the open hatch, a sign that Lieutenant Garland had complied with her requests.

He appeared in the doorway to the garage. "Everything all right?"

Brennan raised a finger in a just-a-moment manner. Then she lay on the floor so she could drop her head through the hole and look around in the crawl-space.

Halogen work lights were placed at intervals along the perimeter, all pointed in one direction, so they looked like they were chasing each other.

Nice, Brennan thought.

By not having them pointed into the middle of the crawlspace, Garland had illuminated the area without forcing Brennan and Wu to stare directly into a lamp every time they turned toward the wall.

Two fans spun at a low setting, moving the air around, but not enough to create mini-duststorms, when the anthropologists began digging.

Withdrawing her head from the hole, she grinned at Garland and gave him a thumbs-up. "Perfect, Lieu-tenant."

He raised a hand to his brow in a small salute. "We aim to please, Doctor. Good hunting. But it may *cost* you. . . ."

"Oh?"

"I have your novel in the car. I want to talk you out of a signature."

Before she could respond, he disappeared.

After dropping through the hole, Brennan took the tools from Dr. Wu before the other anthropologist joined her on the dirt floor.

On their hands and knees, Brennan led Dr. Wu to the exposed portion of hand she had found before.

The Field Museum rep had brought a digital camera and a camcorder, so that every step of the way, they could document what they found.

"You want me to start here?" Dr. Wu asked, through her mask.

"Yes. I'll start at one of the other markers."

But before she did, Brennan paused to watch her colleague.

Dr. Wu snapped a photo, then worked from the small portion of exposed hand, slowly unearthing the rest of the body.

Though they had worked together in the lab, Brennan wanted to see how her counterpart handled herself in the field; and she found Dr. Wu to be as careful and tenacious as herself.

For her part, Brennan started against the opposite wall, slowly working her way down with a small garden trowel.

This was not work for the impatient.

People thought anthropologists and archeologists just stuck a shovel in the dirt, dug around something, popping it out of the earth, dusting it off, then, presto, displaying it in the nearest museum.

That was hardly an accurate portrayal, and when you were digging up a body that had been buried with the idea of keeping it from being discovered by the authorities, the stakes were much higher.

Many of Brennan's peers listened to classical music,

or mastered some breathing method, to keep themselves calm while they plied their trade. Brennan simply concentrated on not missing anything and doing the job with the thoroughness it deserved.

If there were bodies down here, those people might have families who loved and missed them, and had been tortured for months or years or even decades, never knowing what happened to someone precious to them.

Brennan could give those families closure, providing remains for society's rituals of burial and mourning; but more than that, she could help catch the killer who had taken a loved one away.

All she had to do was concentrate, be thorough, and not miss any clues.

Brennan wasn't probing long before she felt the edge of the trowel touch something that was definitely not dirt.

Now she slowed even more, her trowel moving inches at a time. She moved the dirt out of the hole and looked down to see a bare patch of white skin . . .

. . . *the front of a shin, tiny strands of brown hair barely visible in the dirt.*

Jorgensen was apparently still in the serial killer business, despite his age, judging from the remains they had found so far.

Neither of these bodies was far along into decomposition. Brennan was amazed and appalled that a man of seventy—granted, one in phenomenal physical condition—had killed and buried at least two more victims.

Of course, this "old man" had not so long ago nearly dispatched a Chicago cop, an FBI agent, and herself as well. *Feisty,* an adjective she usually associated with active seniors, did not begin to cover William Jorgensen. The only concession he seemed to have made to his declining years was in the mode of his burials: the victims were surprisingly close to the surface.

As she uncovered more of the body, she soon found out why.

The body had been doused with lime.

Brennan knew that many killers who tried to dispose of bodies by burial believed that lime sped up the process of decomposition. She did not know the origin of that particular urban legend, but she knew the exact opposite was true.

Not only did lime not promote decomposition, at shallower depths, like these, lime actually impeded it.

At the end of eight hours, with midnight drawing near, the two anthropologists had exhumed the two bodies they'd been working on, and found signs of three more.

They took a break until daylight, then came back and started again.

And by the end of the day, they had reclaimed the other three bodies, found a sixth, and excavated that as well. Another sweep of ground-penetrating radar confirmed that they had gotten everything.

None of the bodies was reduced to bone, none had been in the ground for more than a couple of years, and although some decomposition was present, these victims all went straight to the coroner for autopsy.

Several things had become clear to Brennan when, for the last time, she left the crawlspace.

William Jorgensen was a serial killer who had been at it for quite some time, six bodies within the last two or three years for sure. Of this there was no doubt.

She and Dr. Wu had excavated all the bodies that were in the crawlspace and yet something did not jibe with this case, in terms of Jorgensen being part of the assembled skeletons that had led them here.

None of the bodies in Jorgensen's house was as old as the bones that had turned up at the FBI and the Biograph.

Where were the other bodies?

Plus she had a sense that she was missing something, something obvious, and this feeling nagged at her like an aching tooth.

These victims of Jorgensen's may have wound up in shallow graves, but the answer to the mystery of the two reconstructed skeletons remained buried deep.

In the yard with Booth and Greene, Brennan watched the loading of the last of the bodies into the coroner's van.

As the vehicle drew away, Dr. Wu approached. She

had removed her coveralls and stood before them in faded jeans and a vintage Rolling Stones tee shirt, looking more groupie than scientist.

"I'm outa here, people," Dr. Wu said. "It's been . . . unique."

Brennan gave the woman a brisk handshake. "Thank you for all your help."

"Thanks for the opportunity to dig in next to you. An honor and a privilege."

Brennan grinned. "Back at ya."

Booth and Greene each shook hands with the doctor, and as she walked away, Greene gave them a wave and followed after her, both casting long shadows in the setting sun.

Soon Brennan and Booth were alone in the yard. The crime scene unit would be going back down into the crawlspace, but Brennan and Booth were done for the day.

She felt both tired and restless. As usual after a hard dig, she craved some alone time. Though she liked Booth, and if pressed would admit to enjoying the man's company, the last thing she wanted to do now was spend an hour in a car with him commuting back to the hotel.

She looked up at him. "Booth, I need a favor."

In the gathering darkness, Booth gazed at her. "Anything."

"Call for a ride, and let me borrow your car."

"Well . . . no."

She glared at him. "Not ten seconds ago, you said, 'anything.' "

"That's why I didn't say *'hell* no.' "

"Give me one good reason, why 'hell no.' "

"For one thing," he said casually, "you don't know your way around this city."

"How would you know whether I do or not?"

"Oh, well, for starters, in the car? Going from the airport to the Biograph? You didn't know squat about Old Town."

"Fine," she said. "I'll call a cab." She turned to stomp off, but he moved and blocked her path.

"Bones! I'll take you anywhere you want to go."

"Look, Booth," she said, her voice icy. "I'm an adult, I have an above-average IQ, and I'm literate enough to read signs and a map. By myself, I found my way to mass graves in Guatemala, Bosnia, and half a dozen other countries around the globe. I don't need *you* to take me *anywhere*."

Booth backed away. "Whoa . . . why so testy all of a sudden?"

She flushed. "Sorry. End of a long day."

"Right. So I'll drop you at your hotel."

He started toward the car, and she moved with him.

Trying not to sound whiny, she said, "I don't want to go anywhere. What I want is some time alone."

He stopped and she stopped and he studied her for a long time without saying anything.

Finally, he reached into his pocket and got out his

cell phone. He dialed a number, his eyes never leaving her face. He wasn't just looking at her—he was looking . . . *deeper* than that.

In fact, his stare was so intense, it made her uncomfortable.

"Woolfolk," he said, "I'm at the Jorgensen house—I need a ride. Come get me."

A pause and squawk from the cell.

Booth frowned. "Just come and get me, all right? That's what partners are for."

Another pause, then Booth clicked off and dropped the cell phone into his pocket. From the other pocket, he withdrew the car keys and handed them to her. "The map's in the glove box."

The keys felt warm in her hand.

"Thank you," she said. "I guess I owe you one."

He nodded. "At least one. . . . Get out of here."

She turned to leave, feeling a little guilty leaving him standing there alone, but knowing that she needed to be by herself right now.

Booth's voice came from behind her. "Pick me up in the morning."

Smiling, she turned and said, "Is that an order?"

He grinned. "Damn straight. I'll be in the lobby at seven a.m. Don't be late."

"Don't you be."

The car started easily and she pulled away from the house, watching Booth watching her leave.

Had his words to Woolfolk—*That's what partners are for*—really been meant for her?

Whatever the case, it felt good to be driving, to be in control, to be alone and to be free.

She drove aimlessly at first, sticking to the surface streets, avoiding the expressway. She rolled down the window, the cool autumn air blowing her hair as she cruised along the long stretches of road.

Out here in the far suburbs, city and country mixed and mingled. She could travel long stretches seeing nothing but shadowy woods, and an occasional set of oncoming headlights.

Other times, the world was mile after mile of big retail stores, restaurants, gas stations, convenience stores, and strip malls filled with coffee shops and other small businesses.

She turned off her brain, let the cool air rush over her, and just drove, forgetting about the bodies, the defacement of the corpses, all of it. Letting go of the sadness that had crept in when she thought of the families these bony reminders of humanity represented.

Then, slowly, her mind turned to other things.

She thought about her friends back in DC, and then various thoughts about Booth traveled through her mind, in particular the case he had been working on here in Chicago, before she arrived . . . searching for the missing informant Stewart Musetti. . . .

And then she had an idea.

7

THE MAP IN THE GLOVE COMPARTMENT LED TEMperance Brennan to Oak Brook, a suburb of high-end stores, businesses, and nine thousand or so citizens.

As she rolled along the road around a ritzy open-air mall, she saw what she was looking for.

Just beyond a Cheesecake Factory loomed a formidable freestanding one-story structure with white stucco walls and an orange tile roof, all meant to put the visitor in mind of the sunny shores of Sicily.

The sign on the front said SIRACUSA.

Famished suddenly—and for some strange reason, just dying for Italian—Brennan pulled into the lot and found a spot for Booth's Crown Victoria.

Even for someone who worked out as regularly as Brennan, opening the restaurant's darkwood door with the wrought-iron handle was like lifting the heavy weights. This conveyed an old-fashioned, the man-gets-the-door mentality that suited the Old World design of the exterior.

Within, that same theme—and vibe—pertained, dark wood and dark support beams and dark-cushioned booths and just plain darkness, with pools of light provided not so much from electricity but the de rigueur red-and-white-checker tablecloths with their red-glass candleholders. The dining room was mostly full, the dinner crowd brisk—a fairly even mix of couples and families.

A partitioned-off bar area to the left seemed largely illuminated by a pair of flat-screen plasmas high behind the counter with the same baseball game playing in silence. The changing lights of the TVs gave the bar an eerie, almost underwater glow.

Frank Sinatra was singing "The Best Is Yet to Come," a little loud for background music, as if the Chairman of the Board (deceased or not) demanded attention.

The attractive, thirty-something hostess—a tall brunette in a crisp white shirt with a tux tie and a black skirt—stood at a low-slung narrow lectern with a seating chart and a reservation book in front of her.

The woman had a ready, if brittle, smile.

"Good evening," the hostess said. "I'm Julia—how many tonight?"

"Just one. Nonsmoking, please."

"Did you have a reservation?"

Brennan shook her head.

Julia swiftly scanned her book, then said, "It'll be a short time before a table is available. You can wait in the bar, if you'd like. Your name?"

"Brennan."

The hostess wrote in her book.

"Julia, maybe you can help me. I heard a friend of a friend works here—Lisa Vitto? Is she on tonight?"

The hostess's smile remained but her eyes tightened. "Friend of a friend? Ms. Brennan, are you by any chance police?"

"No," Brennan said, and affected shock and confusion. "I'm an anthropologist, if it matters."

Julia didn't know what to say to that; her eyes cut to the bar, then returned to Brennan.

"Lisa's a bartender?" Brennan asked.

With a little shrug, Julia said, "You didn't hear it from me. I'll go check on your table now."

As the hostess disappeared into the dining room, Brennan went the other way into the small bar.

A couple sat at one of the dark tables off to the left while two or three middle-aged guys sat at the bar smoking cigarettes, nursing drinks, and watching the ball game joylessly.

The bartender was helped out by a single server, a haggard brunette in her late thirties wearing a white tuxedo shirt, black bow tie, and black slacks; she seemed surrounded by the bar as if life had provided her no way to get out.

Brennan selected one of the tall stools, sitting as far away from the smokers and the couple at the table as she could get.

Down the nearby wall hung framed photographs at various levels—the same two men, perhaps the owners, sometimes both, sometimes singly, were in almost every shot, shaking hands or getting kissed or hugged by presumed celebrities whose grinning faces Brennan mostly didn't recognize.

Slowly, the bartender, who was almost beautiful, worked her way down to Brennan.

The woman had a heart-shaped face with large dark mascara-heavy eyes and a full red-lipsticked mouth; she might have been anywhere from her late twenties to early forties. A few gray streaks highlighted her hair, whether provided by otherwise ineffectual years or the beauty shop, Brennan couldn't say.

She smiled, not at all brittle. "Long day?"

"Oh yeah."

"I'm gonna guess wine."

"Not your first night back there," Brennan said with her own smile. "Chardonnay, please."

"I coulda guessed that, too," the bartender said, and lifted a glass from a shelf behind her before going over to pick out a bottle of wine.

She pulled the cork, poured, and brought the brimming glass down to Brennan. "There you go, sweetie."

The word brought Brennan's friend Angie to mind, and she immediately felt warmth toward this woman.

An illogical response, but after two days digging out skeletons, Brennan would allow herself that.

Putting a twenty on the counter, Brennan kept a finger on it until the bartender tugged on it, then looked at her, still smiling but curious.

"I'll, uh, bring you your change . . ."

Brennan said, "I'm not looking for change."

"What *are* you looking for, honey?"

"Lisa Vitto. . . . Isn't that you?"

The woman's eyes flickered around the bar before returning to Brennan's.

"I can use the twenty," she admitted, in a whisper, "but not the grief. So I will bring you your change, you don't mind."

"Your choice."

When she delivered the change, the bartender said, still whispering, "A female cop, this time? What's the idea coming around the restaurant?"

"I'm not a cop. I'm just hungry. And thirsty." She sipped the wine, but kept her eyes on the bartender. "My name is Temperance Brennan—I'm a forensic anthropologist."

"Well, uh . . . I guess somebody has to be. Whatever that is."

"I'm a scientist. I study bones. I work at a museum, in DC." She shrugged lightly. "So, you know, sometimes I help out the government . . . ?"

The bartender turned, went down to the other end of the bar, gave the game guys some fresh beers, then slowly, seeming to think about it as she wiped the bar, made her way back to Brennan.

"So, then, sometimes you study bones for the FBI," she said, the whisper hoarse and throaty. A guy would have found it sexy; Brennan read it as desperate.

She sipped wine. "On occasion."

"You want to ask about Stewart."

It was not a question.

And "Stewart" was her boyfriend, Stewart Musetti, Booth's missing, presumably abducted witness.

"Yes, Lisa, I would."

She shook her head and dark hairsprayed-shellacked locks bounced, or tried to. "Listen, Ms. Brennan—God knows I'd like to help find Stewart. But I told the FBI everything I know."

"You're *sure*."

Lisa Vitto nodded. "And you *do* know where you are? Who owns this place?"

The Gianellis.

Brennan ignored the question, asking her own: "Do you love him?"

Tears welled in the bartender's eyes and she wiped them away with a napkin she picked up from the edge of the bar; the industrial-strength eye makeup was unaffected. "Yes. I do. But you make it sound like he's alive."

"He might be."

Her eyes were tearing again and she was shaking her head. "From your lips to God's ears."

"Lisa, did you tell the FBI guys that you love Stewart?"

"No."

Casually, she asked, "What else didn't you tell them?"

The glittering eyes tightened. "Honestly, I don't know. I suppose there are things they didn't ask about, but . . . I can't think of a goddamn thing. I mean it."

"Do you have any idea where he is?"

Lisa glanced around the bar again. "Look—I got a couple ideas on that score, but they aren't about where he is."

"I don't follow."

"They're about where his body would be."

"Oh. How about sharing one of those ideas?"

Behind the moisture, the eyes were hard. "I think they gave my guy a ride on the ol' Dunes Express."

"I don't know what that means," Brennan said.

"You don't *want* to know, honey. They killed him, and they buried him. Deep."

"They? You mean the father and son who own this place?"

Lisa just stared at her.

"You think they're behind the death of the man you love, and yet you still work here."

Nodding, Lisa said, "Stewart stood up to them, and

look what that got him. He was brave, I'm not. . . . By staying on here, I show them where I stand."

"That you stand with them, you mean? Not Stewart?"

"That's right, because, honey? Stewart isn't standing at all right now. He's lyin' down . . . and he ain't never ever gonna get up again, much less get back at these boys."

If I can find where he's buried, Brennan thought, *he might. . . .*

"Thank you, Lisa," Brennan said, and she handed the woman a business card with the name and number of her hotel on the back. "If you think of anything, give me a call."

Lisa arched an eyebrow. "If I do, it won't be from here."

But the bartender took the card, slipped it up her sleeve and moved down the bar without another word.

Brennan turned and found a man standing behind her.

"Oh!" she said. "You scared me."

His voice was smooth and resonant. "Didn't mean to. My apologies."

Tall, with dark hair that stood up slightly in the front, the man wore a dark, beautifully tailored suit over a white shirt and geometric-pattern tie, along with dark Italian loafers and a smile that probably made some females swoon but which Brennan found smarmy.

"Are you Ms. Brennan?" he asked.

His voice was smooth as brandy, but about as sincere as twist-cap wine.

"I am," she said.

"Your table is ready," he said, turning to lead her, but then stopped and turned toward her again. "You aren't—*Temperance* Brennan, are you? The writer?"

"Actually, I'm Temperance Brennan the anthropologist. But I have done some writing."

"I should say! A bestseller is *some* writing all right. . . ."

He extended a hand and she had no choice but to shake it.

"Vincent Gianelli," he said, gesturing to himself. "One of the owners of the place."

She had already suspected as much, yet she still fought the urge to snatch her hand back.

"Well," she said. "Pleasure to meet you. I'm in town consulting and one of the guidebooks said Siracusa was the best Italian food in the suburbs."

The handshaking stopped finally. She resisted the urge to count her fingers.

"I like to think best Italian in *Chicago*," he said, and flashed that white smile. "Listen, I'm a big fan— loved your book. Your money's no good here, Ms. Brennan."

"Oh, that's not necessary, Mr. Gianelli."

He held up a stop palm. "It won't be free—it *will*

cost you. . . ." He turned to the bartender. "Lisa! Get the camera!"

"Oh . . . no. . . ."

"Now don't be shy." He took her hand again, and she let him, squirming inside. "We're very proud of our Wall of Fame."

"I noticed. So many celebrities. . . ."

She didn't mention that she hadn't recognized many of them.

"We get all kinds of famous people in here," he said. "My dad knew Frank and Dino, y'know."

Well, even she knew who *they* were. . . .

"Of course," Gianelli was saying, "I was just a kid then . . . but in the years since? Belushi, Aykroyd, anybody who's anybody in Chicago has eaten at Siracusa and become a member of the Wall of Fame."

"Well, that is impressive," she said, and tried to make her smile convey that lie.

"Ditka, Walter Payton, Jordan, Sammy Sosa, you name 'em, they've broke bread here. Even writers like Bill Braschler, Eleanor Taylor Brand . . . and now you."

She swung her head toward the photos to make a show of studying them, even though rarely recognizing any but the most famous on the wall . . . until she saw one photo in the corner, in the shadows.

The photo depicted a balding middle-aged man shaking hands with a much younger Vincent Gianelli.

She recognized the balding man to be John Wayne
Gacy.

One of America's most notorious serial killers
might have been more appropriately displayed on a
Wall of Shame . . . but for some sick reason, there that
notorious killer was, grinning like a demented clown.

"Ms. Brennan. . . . Are you all right?"

"That's . . . that's you shaking hands with John
Wayne *Gacy*, isn't it?"

He grimaced. "Yeah, I know, not the best of taste,
huh? My dad feels the same way—the old boy takes it
down, but I put it back up, then he takes it down, and
I . . . It's almost a running joke between us."

Hilarious, she thought.

"See, the guy, Gacy?" Vincent was saying. "Was real
respectable. I had my picture taken with him when he
was a Chamber of Commerce president or some-
thin'—Nancy Reagan or Jimmy Carter's wife or
somebody, they did the same thing, I think."

"So it's up just as an . . . oddity? A conversation
piece?"

He grinned that hideously handsome smile. "It's
workin', isn't it? Aren't we conversing?"

Vincent pointed to a picture near the bar, showing him in casual clothes, squatting next to a big
tan dog.

"Now, that's my favorite," Gianelli said. "That's me
with Luca, my Neapolitan mastiff."

Brennan nodded approval. How could you abhor an alleged killer who loved dogs?

Wasn't that hard, actually.

Coming up behind them, Lisa said, "Got the camera ready, Vince."

Turning at the sound of the woman's voice, Brennan found herself standing with Vincent Gianelli, his arm around her and shaking her hand.

She thought, *You know what would make an interesting picture?*

And into her mind came the mini-movie of her grabbing Vincent in a wristlock, dropping him to his knees, then crushing his larynx with a martial arts chop. . . .

Of course, in what she laughingly thought of as real life, that might not be the most socially acceptable way for a writer-headed-to-the-Siracusa-Wall-of-Fame to behave herself.

Still, though being this close to Booth's gangster nemesis made her skin literally crawl, she also noticed that her host's expensive cologne wasn't half bad.

What the hell.

She stood stiffly beside him, shaking hands, as Lisa snapped the photo.

The flash blinded Brennan and she saw multicolored spots behind her eyelids. The feeling was just dissipating when she opened her eyes and the flash went off a second time. Again, the colored spots exploded in her vision.

She could barely see Lisa and the camera fading

back toward the bar, though she thought she caught the bartender's smile, which was strained.

"Thank you so much for this," Gianelli said, slipping his arm from her shoulder, but squeezing her hand even harder. "I loved your book so much—*great* read. Let me show you to your table."

Brennan followed along, her vision slowly clearing, her mind still a little blurred.

"You've been really terrific," he said.

"You're welcome. Glad you like the book."

"Oh, I love that kind of stuff—I wore out my copy of *Silence of the Lambs.*"

"Really."

He looked back at her, his dark eyes glittering with enthusiasm. "Yeah, but even before that, from when I was a kid? Always had this fascination with mysteries and crime and horror."

He paused and she almost ran into him as he glanced back to share a whispered secret.

"Especially serial killers," Vincent said.

"No wonder you liked my book," Brennan said, doing something with her mouth that was almost like smiling.

Vincent gave her a real, strangely disarming smile. For a reportedly sociopathic gangster he had a certain charm of sorts.

At a small table by a window onto the parking lot, her host withdrew a chair for her and she took a seat.

But he did not go—he hovered, leaning a hand

against an empty chair beside her, as if hoping she would invite him to join her.

"So," he said, "I suppose you've heard these stupid rumors about my family."

"Rumors?"

He shrugged. "The usual stereotypes—as if every Italian in Chicago is Al Capone."

She decided to pander. "My understanding is that most of the organized crime in this city is in the hands of street gangs, grown older and more savvy."

She was practically quoting a *Chicago Tribune* article she'd read the other day.

But Vincent took the remark at face value. "Exactly! You want to hear something interesting?"

"Sure."

"No one in my family . . . *no one* . . . has ever done time or even been convicted of a felony."

Brennan blinked. ". . . Well. How many families can say that?"

"Right! What are you working on in Chicago? Is it for the FBI or research for a new book?"

She tried to smile again but it felt like a wince; she wondered what it looked like.

"You've been so gracious," she said, "and I don't mean to be rude . . . but, really, that's something I can't talk about."

Vincent patted the air. "It's okay, it's okay . . . business is business. I understand. The feds get nutzoid about leaks."

". . . Thanks for not pressing."

"No problem." Then he leaned in. "But tell me—is it this serial killer thing? The bones at the Biograph?"

Somehow Brennan willed her mouth not to drop open.

She had thought that no one outside of the Booth/Brennan circle knew about the case; but once the Chicago police were in on it, she should have known nothing would remain secret. Too many people were involved for it to stay quiet.

At least the media didn't seem to have it yet.

But Vincent Gianelli did.

"You don't have to answer," Vincent said. "I just figured, with your background? You'd be in on that."

A waiter approached, short, in his early twenties, with swept-back black hair. Like the rest of the wait staff and Lisa the bartender, he wore a white tuxedo shirt, black bow tie, and black slacks.

"This is Hector," Vincent said. "He's our best. He'll be your server."

The young, Hispanic-looking waiter smiled and placed Brennan's glass of wine from the bar on the table. The glass had been refilled.

Despite all this hospitality, she couldn't quite bring herself to ask Vincent to join her—she really didn't feel she had the interrogative skills to pump the man about the missing Musetti without giving herself away.

Besides, Vincent was taking his leave, finally.

"I really do love your writing," he said. "It's so true to life. . . . If you need anything while you're in the area, don't hesitate to call."

Brennan nodded. "Thank you, Mr. Gianelli."

"Vincent. Please. Make it Vincent."

"Thank you, Vincent."

"You're very welcome, Temperance."

As he turned and strode away, Vincent Gianelli seemed very pleased with himself.

Brennan couldn't tell if the mobbed-up restaurateur really was a big fan, or if *he* was pumping *her* for information. He seemed to know what was going on in this city even before the media, so the fact that she was working on a case with Booth might well have been known to him.

On the other hand, she wasn't working on the Gianelli/Musetti case against his family, so what was Brennan to him?

Hector handed her a menu.

"I'll give you a minute to make your selection," Hector said, and disappeared.

When the waiter returned, Brennan made her choice, then nursed the second glass of wine until her food arrived. She ate quickly, and really enjoyed the meal—gangsters or not, the Gianellis knew how to run a restaurant.

As the waiter refilled her cup for a final after-dinner coffee, Brennan asked for the bill.

"On the house," Hector said.

"No, I could never . . ."

Hector waved a hand. "Mr. Gianelli said you would say that. He said to tell you this is standard procedure for celebrities who join our Wall of Fame."

"And did he tell you I would very likely insist on paying no matter what you or he said?"

With a sideways smile, Hector said, "Yes, he did—pretty much word for word."

Brennan assumed she was supposed to find that charming; she did not.

"Hector, please get me the check."

The waiter shook his head. "Normally at Siracusa, the customer is always right; but I learned a long time ago that here? Mr. Gianelli's wishes are *my* wishes."

"*Hec*-tor. . . ."

"I'm sorry, Ms. Brennan—I don't have it."

"Then get me Mr. Gianelli."

"I can't, ma'am. He's left for the evening."

Nonetheless, Brennan tossed two twenties on the table. Perhaps Hector would end up with a hell of a tip, but Brennan could not allow herself to be comped for dinner by the likes of Vincent Gianelli.

She sat in the car, cooling down as she read the map by the light on the ceiling, and picked a route back to the hotel.

As her fingers touched the ignition key, Brennan thought about everything she knew about the mob, the Mafia, La Cosa Nostra; she read mostly non-fiction and had taken in her share of true crime.

But she also thought about *The Godfather,* one of the handful of movies she'd bothered to see in her life.

Remembering the scene where Michael's Italian wife got blown up when she started a car, Brennan felt a momentary chill.

Then she smiled at herself in her rearview mirror, and mouthed, "Silly."

Anyway, she wasn't working on anything mob-related, though, was she? That was Booth's domain.

She had tried to help him out a little by talking to Musetti's girlfriend (though he'd be irritated with her for that). And—just as Booth had told her it would— that had pretty much been a fool's errand.

She turned the key and the Crown Vic roared to life, and she said to herself in the mirror, "See—we didn't blow up."

She swung out of the parking lot, drove a block, got on the expressway, and headed east.

The night was dark but cloudless, with lots of stars and a very white half-moon. Obeying the speed limit, Brennan drove along, enjoying the solitude and freedom.

Although she worked with a good-sized staff at the Jeffersonian, Brennan was basically a loner, and the last few days she had found herself surrounded by other people at every turn.

It felt good just to be alone for a while.

Every now and then a car would pass her, but for this time of night, traffic was scant. When the white

SUV pulled up behind her, Brennan noticed but paid little attention. She assumed it would pass her soon enough.

It didn't.

After a mile or so, she began to get anxious, and was reaching for her cell phone to call Booth when, finally, the SUV pulled around her and passed.

She shook her head and sighed.

This whole thing was starting to get to her.

Two days of excavating the victims of a decades-busy serial killer, then "relaxing" by hanging out with a slick, sick gangster at his restaurant . . . well. No wonder she was exhausted, physically and mentally.

She knew all she needed was a good night's sleep. But she'd wait till she was in bed at the hotel, and not behind the wheel of the Crown Vic, before getting started. . . .

The rest of the trip was uneventful and she turned the car into the hotel garage, grateful the end of this long day was finally in sight. She had found her way home all by herself, which would have no doubt wounded Booth's pride, and was now ready to take a shower and get to bed.

She pulled the Crown Vic into a parking spot in the hotel's parking ramp, got out, and locked the vehicle with the remote on her keys.

Trudging up the level to the elevator at the far end, her purse swung over her shoulder, she passed parked cars on either side of the aisle. As she neared the end, she glimpsed a white SUV.

She stopped and stared at it, fighting the urge to go look in the windows.

Sure, it reminded her of the one that had spooked her on the freeway; but white SUVs were hardly uncommon. . . .

Brennan was walking past the rear of the vehicle when the back door flew open.

Instinctively she threw up her arms, which kept the door from hitting her in the face, but it came at her with such force, she was knocked off balance anyway, and almost went down, staggering back. Her purse flew off her shoulder, skidding under a car behind her.

Three figures in black, each wearing a stocking-cap mask, piled out of the vehicle, coming toward her.

She reacted, kicking one in the chest, but the effort wobbled her farther, and the other two got to her, one on either side.

The first blow, a fist, caught her hard but missed her kidney.

She felt the air rush out as she dropped, and tried to roll, hoping to get some space so she could fight back; but the second guy kicked her in the side of her head, sending bells, sirens, and whistles blaring in her brain.

Her vision blurred as she felt another fist dig into her stomach. The first guy was up now and they had her triangulated. The kicking started again and Brennan made herself as small a target as possible, the blows coming one after the other.

Consciousness fluttered like a dying bird, and Brennan knew she either had to act . . .

. . . or die.

She lashed out with her foot, and swept one attacker off his feet.

As he crashed to the concrete, the others hesitated.

That was the moment she needed.

She drove her fist into the nearest crotch. As the assailant screamed, another one grabbed her head. He was about to drive it into the cement, when she brought her hand up and smashed it into his nose.

The guy released her as he gurgled in pain and stumbled backward.

Every bone in her body hurt, but she struggled to her feet.

But the others were up too.

One pulled an automatic, and as the other two jumped into the SUV, he leveled the pistol at Brennan.

She dove behind a car as he emptied the clip, windows spiderwebbing, metal doors and fenders puckering, one shot ricocheting off the cement, a piece of concrete or bullet nicking her leg.

She looked under the car, trying to see if her attacker was coming at her; but what she saw was her purse.

Grabbing it and dragging it to her, she tore through the contents.

All she came up with was a small, voice-activated mini-cassette player.

Hearing the SUV start, she rose. The vehicle backed out of the parking place, the third guy barely getting in as the driver stomped on the gas and the truck hurtled out of the ramp.

She fired the mini-cassette player at the retreating vehicle, heard the thing *thwack* into the back window of the SUV.

Then the vehicle was gone, and her attackers with it. Unsteady on her feet, struggling to hold on to that fine Italian meal, Brennan fished out her phone and speed-dialed Booth's number, then slumped to the concrete.

In the distance, sirens spoke, and she figured the gunshots had spurred someone to call 911.

"Booth," he said, after the second ring.

"Jumped me," she managed.

"What? Who? *Temperance?* . . . Are you all right?"

She didn't have the strength to answer.

"Where are you? *Temperance!*"

"Hotel," she managed. "Ramp . . ."

Then everything went black .

Brennan was loath to open her eyes.

If her head hurt this much with her eyes *closed*, what the hell would *open* feel like?

She didn't care to find out.

She lay there, doing an inventory of what hurt and what did not.

The "did not" list took considerably less time, involving as it did her toenails, one earlobe, and about one square inch of the area between.

What had happened in the hotel parking garage played through her memory like a sped-up movie; and she knew then that she would have to open her eyes to discover who had found her—the good guys, or the returning bad guys in the SUV. . . .

Opening them a fraction at a time, Brennan finally got her lids parted enough to allow vision; and, much to her surprise, the pain in her head dissipated.

Slightly.

Brennan eased her head to the right and saw a hospital monitor. The numbers showed her blood pressure, normal, and her heart rate, also normal.

Well, at least something in her life was normal.

The pain in her head erupted again, and she had to close her eyes for several long moments before it subsided.

When she opened them again, the pain was not as severe. She continued her visual survey, content that she was in a hospital, which meant the authorities had been the ones to locate her.

The next thing she saw was a big window with the blinds drawn.

Adjusting her near vision, she took stock of a

needle in her right arm and followed the line to a pair of clear plastic bags hanging from a stainless-steel pole. One was saline, the doctors keeping her fluids up, the other a painkiller.

Great.

If it hurt this much while she was on an IV painkiller, what was cold turkey going to feel like?

With considerable effort, Brennan swung her head to the left, seeing a TV mounted on the wall at the foot of the bed. She panned to a dresser on the wall to her left; and beyond that, curled up in an uncomfortable-looking chair, snoring quietly, sprawled Seeley Booth.

Covered with a white hospital blanket thinner than Bill Jorgensen's alibi.

And for a moment or two, she didn't hurt at all.

A voice from the doorway said, "Look who's back among the living."

Brennan turned to see a slender woman in white slacks and a flowered smock.

"I'm Nurse Oakley," the woman said, striding in. "But you can call me Betty."

Looking back to the chair, Brennan saw Booth stirring as the nurse came in and took her pulse.

"How are we feeling?" the nurse asked.

"We are feeling like three guys kicked the hell out of us," Brennan said.

The nurse nodded. "That sounds about right. Pulse is fine—sense of humor, too. . . . I'll tell Dr. Keller you're awake. He'll be in shortly."

The nurse flicked a smile and was gone.

Rubbing the sleep from his eyes, Booth sat up.

"How long have I been out?" Brennan asked.

Booth checked his watch. "Just about twenty-four hours."

Her tongue felt thick. "I'm thirsty."

Booth went to a small bedside table and picked up a plastic cup with a lid and a straw. He held it as she gulped, the icy water tasting wonderful.

"Care to share what happened?" Booth asked.

She told him about her reception in the garage.

"*Three* bastards?" he asked.

She nodded. "Is that an official FBI designation for assailants, Booth? 'Bastards'?"

"Why, how would an anthropologist put it?"

She thought. "Bastards will do."

"Any sort of description?"

Shaking her head, and wishing she hadn't, Brennan said, "Three men wearing stocking-cap masks—all dressed in black. About average height, one a little heavier than the other two, but . . . that's about it."

She was irked that someone whose expertise was bones—who understood posture, stature, kinesiology—could not provide a more detailed description of her attackers.

The bastards, yes *bastards*, had gotten on her so damn fast that her only thought had been survival.

Booth was asking, "The SUV?"

She searched her memory, fuzzy with drugs. "White."

"Did you get the make, model?"

More searching. "No. Sorry. General Motors, maybe?"

"Plate number?"

"Nope."

"Bumper stickers?"

"No, but I did hit the back window with my mini-cassette player."

Booth frowned. "Cassette player?"

"I threw it at them—you know, that little mini thing I use to record interviews and so on." She shrugged and it hurt. "That was all I had."

He was still frowning. "Wasn't a cassette player at the scene."

"Somebody probably picked it up," Brennan said. "Some bystander, 'cause the bad guys were gone. . . . Spoils of war." She had a sudden thought. "What about my purse?"

Booth shook his head. "Sorry. Not at the scene, either."

"Shit," she said.

"Anybody could have picked it up—a good five or six minutes between when you called me and the cops arrived."

Shit shit *shit*.

Her purse, her money (what there was of it), her credit cards, dammit, *all* her ID, gone now.

"My cell phone?"

He nodded and got something out of his pocket.

Her phone.

"This you still have," he said. "Was in your hand."

"Security video?" Brennan asked.

"Yeah," Booth said, "but not much on it—white SUV, picture's crap, couldn't even tell the make and model, let alone catch the license number."

Brennan felt empty inside.

Booth said, "Tell me where you were from the time you left me."

". . . Promise you won't be mad?"

"No," he said.

She began—

"*Siracusa?*" he fumed.

She shrugged, and again it hurt. "I had to eat."

His eyes and nostrils flared. "You—"

"I thought I would lend you a hand."

"Did I *ask* you to?"

"No," she said, defensive. "But you said Lisa Vitto hadn't been interviewed by a policewoman, so I thought I'd give it a try."

"With *your* people skills?"

She almost said, *Look who's talking.*

But she knew he was right.

Lamely she managed, "Sorry."

"And did Lisa Vitto tell you anything she didn't tell me?"

"Just that she loved Stewart Musetti."

"She didn't have to," Booth said. "It was obvious she loves him."

"I said 'loved.' It was more past tense. She's convinced he's dead."

Booth said nothing.

Brennan thought about it a moment and said, "You know how you always say I don't get out enough?"

"What, we're changing the topic to the obvious now?"

She ignored that and said, "You continually make fun of me not understanding or knowing about any pop culture references. . . ."

"Of course."

"Well, Lisa mentioned that she thought 'they'—I assume she meant the Gianellis—put her guy Stewart on the 'Dunes Express.' "

Booth shook his head. "I don't know what that means."

"Are you mocking me?"

"No. I don't know what the hell that means."

She sighed, and the IV must have kicked in, because it didn't hurt at all. "Well, at least it's not just me this time."

"One good thing," Booth said. "This narrows the list of suspects who attacked you."

"How?"

"Had to be the Gianellis. Their crew. I mean, Vincent saw you talking to Lisa."

She frowned at him. "But *you* talked to Lisa, didn't you? He didn't come after you."

"They tend not to frontally assault FBI or cops. You're sort of a civilian."

"But why would he come over and talk about being a big fan and . . . what's the word? Shmoo with me?"

"Shmooze."

"Why would he do that, and then send his boys after me?"

Booth shrugged. "Maybe he was stalling you while some underling rounded up the goon squad and piled them into a white SUV."

". . . Couldn't it have been a simple mugging?"

"Doubtful."

"Does Jorgensen have any known associates?"

"Are you kidding?" Booth said. "Elderly serial killers don't usually have crews of strong-arms on call."

"But he *is* an elderly serial killer who preys on much younger men, then buries them. . . . He could have had help."

"Bones, he almost took out the three of us by himself!"

Brennan said, "Given . . . but who would consider me a threat? Gianelli, whose case I'm not working? Or Jorgensen, whose basement I'd been excavating for the last two days?"

He was shaking his head again. "Serial killers have been known to work in pairs—but in fours?"

A very tall, very young man in a lab coat and tan Dockers strolled in carrying a chart in front of him like a schoolbook. He wore wire-frame glasses and his hair was straight and dark.

Cheerfully professional, he asked, "And how are we feeling today, Dr. Brennan?"

With that baby face, he looked to be barely out of his teens, much less medical school.

"Lousy," she said. "But good enough to resent everybody using the editorial 'we' about my pain."

"Sorry," he said, and managed a smile. "I'm Dr. Keller."

Booth gave him a look, turned to Brennan, and whispered, "Doogie Howser to the rescue."

She shook her head. "I don't know what that means."

Keller apparently did, and shot daggers at Booth. "I'm perfectly qualified to attend to Dr. Brennan."

"How old are you?" Booth asked. "Twelve?"

"Twenty-seven," the young doctor said. "If it matters."

"Don't mind him," Brennan said to the physician. "Intellect intimidates him."

"Well, there's nothing challenging to understand here." Keller opened her chart and read aloud. "Concussion, two cracked ribs, lacerated ankle, assorted bumps, bruises, scrapes. Bottom line, Dr. Brennan, is you're going to be fine. After a couple days of bed rest, you should be good to go."

Booth's cell phone chirped.

Dr. Keller frowned. "Visitors are required to turn off their cell phones. You—"

The FBI agent waved and disappeared into the hall, closing the door as he left.

The doctor gave her a quick exam and, by the time he was done, Booth was reentering the room.

"Got to go, Bones."

"Not without me, you don't!"

Booth smiled. "You *are* feeling better. Look, this case has gotten weirder."

"Is that possible?"

"Seems to be. We've got Jorgensen in custody, but another skeleton's just turned up. I'm headed out there."

Brennan sat up, wide-eyed. "You mean, *we're* headed out there. . . ."

Dr. Keller said, "Dr. Brennan—"

"My clothes?" she asked Booth, ignoring the physician.

"In the closet," the FBI agent said. "But look, I can handle this. You need to—"

"It's another skeleton. That's where I come in, right? Why you called me in the first place?"

"Well, yeah, sure, but—"

Dr. Keller said, "I really must insist . . ."

Brennan pointed to the IV in her arm. "Would you take this out, Doctor, or should I?"

The young doctor shook his head. "I can't. You've sustained injuries. . . ."

She yanked out the IV needle and blood squirted, and Booth made an *ick* face as she grabbed her sheet and used it as a compress.

The physician was aghast. "Dr. Brennan!"

Staring at the young man, she said, "You have three choices, as I see it. A., you can try to stop me and I'll kick your ass."

Eyebrows hiked, Booth looked at the doctor. "She can do it too, Doogie."

"B., you can call security, but I'll be gone before they get here. Or C., you can bandage this and help me depart with dignity."

Still shaking his head, Keller said, "Dr. Brennan, I'm afraid . . ."

Booth laid a hand on the doctor's shoulder. "Doc, you know who Sisyphus is?"

The doctor blinked. "Uh . . . Corinthian king so cruel that when he went to Hades, his punishment was to roll a rock up a hill and when he got it to the top, roll it back down again?"

Nodding, Booth said, "Surprisingly good lit chops for a medical school grad. So when I tell you that arguing with Bones here is a Sisyphean task, you *do* know what I mean?"

Brennan gaped at Booth, who added, "You think you're the only one who went to college, Bones?"

"Not now," she said, smiling.

Dr. Keller gathered some bandages and tended to Brennan's self-inflicted wound on her IV arm.

While the physician was doing that, Brennan used her free hand to grab her cell phone from the bedstand and call Angela.

"What's up, sweetie?"

Brennan explained, in terse terms, what had happened to her.

Angela was frantic. "My God—are you all right?"

"You *always* ask me that," Brennan said.

"Being your friend always *requires* it!"

"I need you to go to my apartment."

"Because?"

"You're the only one who knows where my security stuff is, and can cancel my credit cards."

Angela's tone grew more serious. "Oh. 'Cause of your purse and . . . well, sure, I'll take care of it right away."

"Thanks."

Brennan ended the call.

Less than half an hour later, she and the FBI agent were racing to the site of the latest skeleton.

8

GLANCING OVER AT BRENNAN—WHO WAS GAZing out her passenger window, lost in private thoughts —Seeley Booth couldn't help but think that maybe he should have fought on the doctor's side and insisted she stay in that hospital bed.

Right now her skin—usually aglow with life— appeared sallow, and tiny beads of sweat glistened on her forehead.

"You okay?" he asked.

She looked his way, gave him a tiny smile and one tired nod. "Yeah. Where was this latest skeleton found?"

"Spring Lake Forest Preserve. On Highway 62."

"And where is that, exactly?"

"Northwest suburbs, Barrington Hills."

Brennan had been in Northwestern Memorial Hospital downtown; this, Booth knew, meant a long trip along I-90 West.

The FBI agent drove fast, but did not have the lights flashing or siren blaring as he wove in and out of Chicago traffic, using all three westbound lanes as he hustled toward the scene. Wrestling with both rush-hour traffic and driving into the setting sun, Booth got off I-90 onto I-290 and, at the very next exit, caught Highway 62.

Booth knew, under normal circumstances, Brennan would be brimming with questions. But he also knew she was recovering her balance—mentally, physically, emotionally—and he would follow her lead.

Step at a time.

The road was only two lanes as they neared their destination, and the surrounding countryside was mostly trees, the occasional house. The sun filtered through the canopy of leaves and Booth felt like he was driving in a tunnel. He took off his sunglasses . . . not that it helped.

He knew they were headed for a forest preserve, but it never failed to amaze him how there could be large rural stretches within the confines of a metropolitan area that was home to millions.

"Who found it?" Brennan asked.

She seemed to be getting up to speed.

"Hikers. They used a cell phone to call the police."

"How did you learn about it?"

"After Jorgensen's house, the cops will call us if they dig up so much as a Milk Bone."

"Milk Bone?"

"Dog biscuit." He glanced at her. "Do you even *own* a TV?"

"Yes," she said blankly, apparently too numb to rise to the bait.

He decided to kid her out of her state—gently. "Ever turn the thing on?"

She hesitated.

"I thought so," he said.

"No . . . I was just thinking. Weather Channel, Discovery, History, A & E, lots of stuff. I just don't have a high tolerance for nonsense."

He'd noticed.

But he was relieved she was alive again.

They lapsed back into silence, Brennan obviously still fighting the effects of the painkillers; and—as they rode along on the tree-sheltered two-lane, going slower now—she nodded off, head against the window.

He let her rest.

Before long, Booth turned into the Spring Lake Forest Preserve parking lot.

A county deputy stood next to a Sheriff's Department car at the entrance, stopping anyone who tried to enter. As Booth swung in, the deputy held up a hand; even though the sun had not set completely, the country law enforcement officer brandished a flashlight in his other hand, careful to aim the beam away from Booth's eyes . . . but waving it so Booth could not miss seeing him.

Booth knew cops felt safer going through an unknown doorway than doing traffic duty.

He stopped and powered down the window as the sentry approached. By the time the deputy got to the door, Booth had pulled out his ID.

"Special Agent Booth and forensic anthropologist Dr. Brennan."

The deputy—medium height, emotionless steel-gray eyes—pointed to several cars parked to the left side of the gravel parking lot.

"Put it over there. No road beyond the lot. Have to walk in."

Booth nodded. "Where's our skeleton?"

"I'll get you a guide," the deputy said. He pushed a button on his shoulder-mounted radio mic. "Bobby?"

He waited.

Finally, a voice said, *"Yeah?"*

"Carl. Come on out—FBI Special Agent and an anthropologist. Need you to show 'em to the cemetery."

"On my way."

Deputy Carl and Booth exchanged nods, then Booth pulled the Crown Vic around and parked.

Booth hurried around the vehicle to help his partner, but Brennan was already wobbling out.

When he caught up to her, she leaned against him

and he helped her straighten up, then she took a long breath, held it, and expelled it.

Guilt flushed Booth's face. "I should never have let you talk me into this."

"I'm all right," she said, pulling away from him. "Really."

He kept a hand near her, but didn't touch her. He knew to give her her space. This was a woman who took pride in her independence, and he respected that. Admired it, even.

Still, he asked, "You sure, Bones?"

"Dead sure—we've got work to do."

Booth was looking for something else to say, when a flashlight beam cut through the darkness. A deputy sheriff trailed the shaft of light into the parking lot.

"Welcome to Spring Lake Forest Preserve," the deputy said, pleasant but not cheerful. He was a blocky blond with dark blue eyes in an oval, pug-nosed face; Booth made him in his early twenties.

"Thanks for having us," Booth said. "You Bobby?"

"Yeah."

"I'm Booth. This is Dr. Brennan."

No handshakes, just nods.

The deputy said, "I'll lead you down the path to the cemetery where the thing was found."

"Appreciate it," Booth said.

Deputy Bobby was shaking his head. "Weirdest thing I ever saw around these parts. . . . You folks watch your step, now. It's gettin' pretty dark and these roots and stuff along the way? You can trip and take a header, easy."

Swell, Booth thought.

Here he was dealing with a half-conscious Brennan—okay, maybe a ninety-percent conscious Brennan—and now they were traipsing through the woods in the dark.

Though the glow of the city and the suburbs surrounded the area, the woods were darker than anyplace Booth had been since his military days. The only light beyond the deputy's flashlight came from the moon and a few scattered stars.

Whatever sense of wonder, of the majesty of the universe, that others might feel in the Great Out of Doors had been ruined forever for Seeley Booth. The woods to him were jungle, and jungle meant memories of the time he spent as a sniper.

Deputy Bobby led the way, single file, Booth behind Brennan to catch her if need be. The path was well worn and mostly flat, leaves falling in heavy clumps in some places, making exposed roots even harder to see despite Bobby trying to point them out with the beam of the flashlight.

Trailing behind, feeling sweat starting to soak the underarms and back of his shirt, Booth was beginning to wonder how Bobby had made it to the parking lot in such a short time after the radio call.

Then the woods parted and Bobby stepped left, and

Brennan right, and Booth found himself damn near face-to-face with the eyeless sockets of a skull, the rest of the skeleton hanging down as if the fleshless man stood before him.

The arms of the skeleton had been draped over and secured to the wrought-iron gate of the Guild Cemetery. Like the first skeleton, this one had been wired together in the manner of those seen in medical school classrooms.

Booth stepped to one side and got his bearings.

Small, at least by modern standards, the cemetery was home to one hundred or so souls buried between 1854 and 1899. The wrought-iron fence that surrounded the space seemed in good repair, but the gate was padlocked and Booth knew that this final resting place received few visitors these days.

At least until tonight.

Now, besides Bobby, two more uniformed sheriff's department officers, as well as Special Agent in Charge Dillon and SA Woolfolk had come to pay their respects, before Booth and Brennan even arrived.

Inside the fence, Booth saw a flashlight beam, moving slowly between the graves.

"Crime scene unit on the way?" Booth asked Bobby.

The deputy turned to the older of the two uniformed officers. "Sheriff, this FBI agent here wants to know if the—"

"My hearing's fine, Bobby," the sheriff said, stepping forward and meeting Booth's eyes. "And yes, crime scene analysts are coming—I requested Chicago PD and got it. I'm Sheriff Greg Trucks, by the way."

The sheriff—a beefy, craggy, dark-haired guy in his fifties—extended a hand.

Booth shook it, introducing himself and Brennan.

"Glad to have you, Doctor," Trucks said to Brennan, shaking her hand as well. "We haven't had a murder in seven or eight months . . . and we *never* had anything like this."

"Where are you," Brennan asked, "with checking the graves themselves?"

Trucks pointed toward the nearby cemetery. "That's Mary Newman in there—she's from the local library association. They've taken on the history of the cemetery as a pet project, so I called her in. She'll know if anything's been disturbed."

While they waited for Ms. Newman to finish her survey, Booth watched Brennan studying the skeleton in the moonlight.

After a short time, she turned to the deputy.

"Bobby? May I borrow your flashlight?"

Bobby glanced at his boss; the sheriff nodded.

The young deputy handed over the light and Brennan ran the beam slowly up and down the limbs of the skeleton.

The other onlookers seemed as fascinated as Booth

as they watched her work the beam over the skull, the ribs, then the spine, and, finally, the legs clear down to the feet . . .

. . . where there appeared to be another note bound to the toes.

Turning to the sheriff, she asked, "Have you photographed this site?"

Trucks nodded. "But I don't think we should be touching any of it until the crime scene people get here."

That, Booth knew, was the wrong thing to say to Brennan, drugged or not.

"Thank you for the advice, Sheriff," she said, artificially polite. "My advice to you, had I had the opportunity to offer it earlier, would've been not to have all these people tromping around a crime scene. I didn't *plan* on touching anything—I was merely requesting information."

She's baaaack, Booth thought, and almost smiled.

The sheriff, who looked like he'd been slapped, struggled for a response.

Before this could escalate into an argument, Booth's local boss, Dillon, stepped in, but his words were addressed to neither the sheriff nor Brennan.

"Ms. Newman," he said, "what did you find?"

Booth looked up to see a woman leaning on the fence near the gate. Tall, thin, with a sharp chin and a straight nose that propped up wire-frame glasses, white hair flying out from under a Cubs baseball cap, the chipper Ms. Newman wore a Cubs windbreaker and jeans.

Booth couldn't see the woman's eyes in the darkness, but she seemed to be smiling.

"Everything's all right," she announced with obvious relief, as if a skeleton wasn't tethered to the fence barely two feet from her. "Not a single grave has been tampered with."

"Mary, you're *sure*?" Trucks asked.

"Gregory, why would you even ask?" She tried to respond with grace, but the irritation was evident. "You know this place has been my life for the last ten years."

"Sorry, Mary," Trucks said, suitably cowed. The beefy guy was not doing well with the "weaker" sex tonight.

Five minutes later the Chicago PD crime scene unit finally showed up and started working the scene. The parking lot had been disturbed by ten or so city, county, state, and federal cars since the perp had made his delivery, but a couple CSUs stayed behind to work the lot anyway.

This assumed, of course, that the perp had arrived by car and hiked in as they had. Airlifting was probably the only other way, and no one in their right mind would skydive with an extra skeleton lashed to his or her back.

Not that leaving reassembled skeletons around Chicago indicated a right mind. . . .

Booth noticed Brennan shining the flashlight on the skeleton again.

"What's up?" he asked.

Aiming the beam at the midsection of the skeleton, Brennan said, "Look at this. What do you see?"

Booth stepped closer. "Bones, I see bones."

"Cute," she said. "But don't just take in the surface—look closer."

He tried, but gave up. "I honestly don't know what I'm supposed to be looking for . . ."

"Try here," she said, pointing to where the clavicle met the sternum just above the ribs.

"Yeaaaaah," he said, still not getting it.

"Do you see the dirt spots on the ribs?"

"That I do see. Why?"

"*Where* are they on the clavicle?"

She shined the light on the collarbone and he searched for any kind of smudge but saw nothing.

"There isn't any dirt on the clavicle," he said. "Okay. What's that mean?"

"*This* bone . . . this *particular* bone . . . has never been buried . . . and judging from the color? It was defleshed artificially."

He repeated, not quite sure it was English: "Artificially defleshed . . . ?"

"Yes. Sometimes, in the lab, if we have a partial body and we want to study *just* the bones, we will deflesh the bone by soaking the remains in enzyme-activated detergent and water."

"And I thought my job had its gross moments," Booth said.

"It's just science, Booth. What if defleshing bones meant the difference between finding a murderer and not?"

"As long as the bones getting defleshed isn't *you*, Bones? I'd say deflesh away . . . but it's still gross."

Booth turned to find that their exchange had garnered an audience.

Upon being noticed, the others backed off a little. Booth looked past the crowd to see members of the crime scene unit trudging toward them, kits in hand.

He found himself instinctively shielding Brennan, who was in the process of using tweezers to put something in a tiny plastic bag, which she slipped into her pocket.

When the leader of the CSU team, a tall, rangy brown-haired guy named Lieutenant Platt, had met everyone, Brennan explained that she and Booth wanted the skeleton as soon as possible.

Pratt said, "Dr. Brennan, we've got the word on you from Lieutenant Greene."

She blinked. "You do?"

"We do. He said you're tops and anything you ask for, we should give to you. Expect nothing but cooperation here."

She smiled. "Cool."

The crime scene unit went to work and, an hour later—even though there was much to be done at the scene—Platt released the skeleton to Booth and Brennan.

"Where's the note?" Booth asked.

"Well," Pratt said, "we kept that, of course."

"We'll need it."

"You said the skeleton, that's what you got."

"And everything that went with it—including the note."

Pratt grimaced, then forced a smile. "Agent Booth, I indicated to Dr. Brennan we'd cooperate. This is a joint investigation. But this is still my crime scene. I've turned over the skeleton, and that will have to do for now."

SAC Dillon came over and, pleasantly professional, said, "This is a federal investigation, Lieutenant. We'll handle the note, and send you a copy with a full report on our findings."

Pratt frowned.

He was just about to reply, apparently not in a nice way, when Brennan approached the crime scene investigator and said, "We're wasting time, struggling over turf. You were great about the skeleton, and I appreciate that. But we need some more of that cooperation you promised."

Pratt shook his head, only it wasn't a refusal, because he immediately had one of his techs fetch the note and bring it to Booth.

This latest missive from their skeleton assembler was now safely sealed inside a plastic evidence bag.

"Thank you for your cooperation," Dillon said to Pratt, and walked away.

Brennan smiled sweetly at the already put-upon crime scene investigator and asked, "Just one more thing?"

Pratt laughed. "Not my firstborn? My wife will have a fit."

"No. Not that. We could use some large evidence bags to convey the skeleton safely. Could we borrow some?"

"And by 'borrow,' you mean 'have'?"

"Yes."

Soon Booth and Brennan were utilizing large plastic bags from the crime scene unit, slipping them over the skeleton. The entire thing was covered with plastic by the time they loaded it into the backseat of the Crown Vic.

As they pulled back onto the road, Booth phoned Dr. Wu, who, despite the late hour, agreed to meet them at the Field Museum ASAP.

Booth ended the call, passed through a T-intersection and headed east back toward the expressway. He shot Brennan a glance and noted her puzzled expression.

"What?" he asked.

"I know I've been taking painkillers, but I thought you said this was Highway 62."

"It is," Booth said, pointing to a sign they were passing.

"Then why did the sign back there say this is Algonquin Road?"

"Because it is. Highway 62 is Algonquin Road."

Booth tried to keep his eyes on the road, but he kept glancing over at Brennan, who was obviously pondering something.

When he couldn't take it anymore, he finally said, again, "What?"

"Something doesn't fit."

"How so?"

"We've been working with the assumption that Jorgensen was the one placing the skeletons, right?"

"Right. And we caught him."

"But the last one didn't turn up until *after* he was in custody."

"Also correct, but that doesn't mean that he didn't stage it, before we caught him. Plenty of opportunity for him to do that, and it was only found just now."

"Possible," she said. "But think about it. Where was the first skeleton discovered?"

"At the Dirksen Building."

"Why there?"

"To get our attention."

Brennan nodded. "Which it did."

"Yeah."

"What about the second skeleton?"

He hit the exit and they were on the expressway now. Traffic was thin, the hour late, the lights of the city making Booth feel a part of civilization again. "By the Biograph theater."

"But the homeless witness, ultimately, led you to where?"

"Jorgensen's old haunts, his old house."

"And now?"

Booth shrugged.

"Algonquin Road?"

"So?"

"Where did Jorgensen live?"

Seeing where she was going now, Booth said, "Algonquin."

Forehead creased, she asked, "Would he *be* that obvious?"

"Sure, if he wanted to get caught badly enough."

Brennan shook her head. "I don't think so. You were in that kitchen. Did he *behave* like he wanted to be caught?"

"Maybe it was a . . . go-out-in-a-blaze-of-glory deal."

"Booth, he didn't act like he wanted to die. To take us with him. He wanted to *survive*. Which he did."

"Creeps do weird things, Bones. This is my area, trust me—serial killers do things and sometimes don't even know they're doing it."

She said nothing, staring straight ahead.

Booth kept trying: "He picks the cemetery, for some completely other reason, not even thinking about what road it's on . . . but subconsciously, he's trying to get caught, right? So out of all the cemeteries in Chicago, he picks the one on Algonquin Road."

She wasn't buying. "It's not logical."

"Neither is killing young men and burying them in your crawlspace or making 'new' skeletons out of the pieces of those people. Serial killing isn't about logic. . . . It's just a part of their sicko M.O."

"I still think we're missing something," Brennan said.

"If it'll make you feel better, have an advance peek at the note. Maybe there's something there."

She got the evidence bag out, turned on the dome light, smoothed the plastic so she could read the latest missive. ". . . All in caps again. . . ."

"What does it say?"

" 'To the FBI,' " she read. " 'I've given you two chances already and you are proving to be as incompetent as the police. How much easier do I need to make it for you? I've given you every clue, every possibility to make it as easy for you as I can. Still, you are incompetent, inept, and unable to catch me. My patience is wearing as thin as your pathetic skills. Perhaps I need to just send you my name and address, like the police, that is probably the only way you will ever darken my door.' Signed, 'Nerd.' "

"'Nerd?' As in *'Revenge of the . . .'*?"

"I don't know what that means," she said. " 'Nerd' as in N-E-R-D."

"Three notes, three different signatures," Booth said. "Now that really doesn't make sense. . . ."

Brennan turned off the dome light. "Imagine we'd found this skeleton prior to pinpointing Jorgensen."

"Why would that make a difference?"

"I'd have made the same Algonquin Road connection, and so would you. . . . Would Jorgensen make it so easy to track him? While using three different names that have nothing to do with him?"

"Bones, again—you keep using logic to try to explain an illogical act. You'll never get anywhere that way."

"Notebook and pen?"

He squinted at her.

"Eyes on the road," she said. "Do you have a notebook and pen?"

Driving with one hand, and digging in his pocket with the other, he searched for the small notebook and ballpoint; he found them and handed them over.

Brennan, very quiet now, began writing something. Focused. Gone somewhere in her mind and not inviting him along.

Booth used the drive time to think about what he would do about the Musetti case once this Skel craziness was over. Which, he told himself, should be in the very near future.

The suspect was in custody, the evidence piling up.

Nothing was directly tied to Jorgensen, but that would come soon enough.

And that job would be for squints like Brennan.

She was still scribbling when he got off the interstate and wound his way over to Lake Shore Drive, which he followed south to the Field Museum. He parked near a back door with a single security light.

Dr. Wu wasn't there yet and they would be waiting awhile, so he asked, "What's in the little bag you spirited away at the scene?"

"The little bag in my pocket?"

"*That* little bag."

"A hair I found stuck in one of the knots used to assemble the skeleton. I'll send it to Jack to identify."

Then, as if they hadn't even spoken, Brennan went back to working on whatever she was doing in the notebook, and Booth returned to devising new ways to attack the Musetti search.

Brennan suddenly grunted something that was almost a laugh, and a self-satisfied one at that.

"An anagram," she said.

"What is?"

"The signatures. They comprise an anagram."

"The three signatures do?"

"The three signatures. If you rearrange the letters of the names, here is what you get."

Booth met Brennan's excited eyes, then looked down at the notebook in the meager glow from the security light coming through the windshield.

In Brennan's sharp printing was one word:

MASTERMIND.

Booth started mentally rearranging the letters himself now, not wanting to be one-upped by a squint.

"Could be Mister Damn," he announced.

She stared at him, an eyebrow arched, and he immediately realized how dumb he sounded.

"All right," he said finally. "Yours probably makes more sense."

"You think?"

Before he could get any more embarrassed, Booth noticed Dr. Wu's Volvo pulling into the lot. He glanced over at Brennan, still giving him that arched eyebrow expression.

He held up his hands in surrender.

"Mastermind it is," he said.

As Dr. Wu unlocked the Field's rear door, Booth and Brennan got their newest skeleton's worth of evidence out of the back and carried it into the lab.

They rested it on the central table, removed the plastic bags, and Brennan put on a lab coat and gloves. Dr. Wu did the same, and then the two women examined the skeleton while Booth hovered and tried to look like he wasn't.

Dr. Wu concurred with Brennan's defleshing theory and again both women were convinced that the bones had come from more than one body.

"The clavicle and ribs are from different bodies,"

Brennan told Booth. "I explained that to you at the scene."

He nodded.

"The pubic symphysis belonged to a young man while the closure of the sutures in the skull belong to a much older man."

"Either of those belong to the others?"

"Maybe, but the clavicle, several of the hand bones, and the legs below the knees probably all came from the same person."

"And those, you think, are more recent?"

"In terms of time since death," she said, "yes."

"Where does that leave us?"

Brennan smiled. "More information is more knowledge. More knowledge gets us closer to the identity of the bastard sending us these sick messages."

"Makes sense. Makes damn good sense."

"We'll package this one up, and you can ship it off to the Jeffersonian."

Booth eyed her curiously. "What are you going to be doing?"

She looked very tired, very pale, and sweat glistened on her forehead again. "I think there's a very good possibility that I'll be sleeping in."

He gave her half a grin, and she gave him the other half.

Then she crumpled. The only thing that kept Brennan from hitting the ground was Booth catching her.

"Better call 911," he told Dr. Wu.

Alarmed, Dr. Wu asked, "Is she going to be all right?"

Booth laid Brennan gently on the floor. "I think she just overdid it. But we better make damn sure."

Dr. Wu was studying him even as she got the cell phone to her lips.

"You really care about her, don't you?" Dr. Wu asked with the faintest trace of a smile.

"Why shouldn't I?" Booth said. "She's my partner."

9

For the second day in a row, Temperance Brennan woke up in a hospital bed.

Which was, let's face it, getting a little discouraging, and not just from a health standpoint.

Brennan might not be the most girly girl around, but having no purse distressed her, and she had been wearing the same clothes for . . . *how* long was it now?

She tried to think back to the last time she had been in her hotel room, but the results were fuzzy.

No shower in at least two days and, since her purse was stolen, she hadn't even been able to comb her hair. She checked beside her to see the saline bottle, the line, the needle; hooked up again, and not in the date sense—at least no painkillers seemed part of the mix, this time.

On top of all that, her cell phone was nowhere in sight, and she had no idea where it was, which meant she was *really* cut off from her life.

Another week in Chicago and she'd be lucky to have the clothes on her back (which, at the moment, were not on her back or any part of her, for that matter).

And this time, Booth wasn't in a chair watching over her, as he had been before, which gave her a pang.

She was alone.

TV was off. Clock said eight a.m.

Breakfast would be around soon and, hospital food or not, that was a good thing, starved as she was.

Her cell phone rang, as if to announce its presence after all, and with childish excitement she recovered it in the folds of her sheets. She snatched it up and hit the button, fast: she knew cell phones weren't permitted in here, and figured Booth must have stowed hers away for her, in the bedclothes, so she would at least have that.

She felt suddenly grateful to the absent Booth, and the feeling wasn't bad at all. . . . Or was she still on painkillers?

Her phone said, "Sweetie, you there?"

"Sorry, Angie—I'm here."

"And where is 'here' today?"

"The hospital again."

"Are you all right?"

The eternal question.

"Just overdid it, Angie. Checked myself out yesterday, little overeager. Must've passed out at the museum. A blink ago I was there, and now I'm here, back in a hospital bed. Seems to be the next morning. . . . What day is it, anyway?"

Angela told her, and relief swept over her.

"Oh," Angela was saying, "and I got your credit cards canceled. No prob. When you get back? We can take care of the rest of your ID and stuff."

More relief.

"Thanks. You're a saint."

"That's not a commonly held opinion, sweetie. Hey, we're finally making progress on the two skeletons you were so kind as to send."

"That's better medicine than this hospital can give me. Spill!"

"I've e-mailed you JPEGs of the 3-D images I've made from the skulls. You *do* still have your laptop, don't you?"

"In my hotel room, I do—assuming I still have a hotel room. . . . What about dental ID?"

"Both of the skeletons—"

"Oh! Before I forget, there are three now. The latest skeleton should be on its way to you today."

Angela sang, " *'It's raining men. . . . '* "

"I don't know what that means."

"Get well, finish your case, come home, and maybe I'll explain it to you."

"Angie—back to the dental IDs."

"I already e-mailed that stuff, too. But here's what we have so far: one skull belonged to a guy named David Parks. Went missing in 1959."

"Who was he?"

"Police didn't want to give me anything. They told me to have Booth ask for the file."

"Interesting."

"I thought so. So pass it along to that good-looking guy you work with."

"I will. Now, who is he?"

"Seeley Booth! He's that hunky agent you—"

"Angie—who is David *Parks*? The owner of the skull in question?"

Brennan knew her friend well enough to know that Angela wouldn't be satisfied with being stonewalled by the cops, and she had the computer chops to get around it.

"Knowing that he disappeared in 1959," Angela said, "I did some digging online. 'David Parks' isn't 'John Smith,' but it's still a pretty common name."

"But you found . . . ?"

"Some old newspaper articles that said Parks was an accountant who had his own business. Then, one fateful night? Dave just fell off the planet."

"That's *it*?"

"According to what the Net gave up, police back in '59 had no leads—everybody in Parks's circle of friends, all *male*, by the way, were suitably distraught."

"You find it significant that all of his friends were male?"

"Just that he had no wife, no girlfriend, no women in his life at all."

Brennan was frowning. "And from this you extrapolate he was gay? How many men in 1959 had tons of gal pals?"

Angela, not at all defensive, said, "Didn't you say your serial killer was targeting gay men, even back then? Seemed worth noting."

"It is. Still, there's no empirical proof that Parks was homosexual."

"Sweetie, there's seldom empirical proof that *anybody* is *anything*."

Brennan couldn't argue with that. "What else?"

"Nothing for Parks. Information was pretty sketchy. Long time ago . . . but that wasn't quite as true for the other skull."

"Who was he?"

"A small-time mobster named Johnny Battaglia."

The back of Brennan's neck prickled.

Angela was saying, "He disappeared in the fall of 1963, leaving behind a wife and two daughters and an arrest record the length of the lakefront."

"Probably *not* gay," Brennan said.

"You never know," Angela said, a shrug in her voice. "But didn't you say Booth was investigating the Gianelli crime family, before you got there?"

The prickly neck was gone but an uneasy queasiness had seeped into her stomach. "Yes. Till our cobbled-together skeletons rudely interrupted him."

"Well," Angela said, "Battaglia allegedly worked with Raymond Gianelli's father back in the forties and fifties."

"I don't see what this has to do with our skeletons," Brennan said.

"Nobody on this end has any ideas, either; but we're still working on that and DNA identification of the other bones."

"Did you copy the Parks and Battaglia info to Booth?" Brennan asked.

"Yes—he's had them awhile."

"Good."

A female orderly arrived bearing a tray with a cup of coffee, a glass of juice, a covered bowl, and a covered plate. Right behind her came a blond nurse in a flowered smock and white slacks.

"You're not supposed to be using a cell phone inside the hospital, Dr. Brennan."

The wide blue eyes and straight-lipped frown made the nurse look serious but not quite cross.

What is this, Brennan thought, *an airplane?*

"Gotta go," Brennan told Angela, and rang off.

She sat quietly while the nurse checked her vitals.

"Feeling better?" the nurse asked, giving Brennan a little smile.

She had to admit, she did feel better; maybe the hospital had been the best place to spend the night, even though she longed to get reacquainted with that hotel room.

"Dr. Keller will be by to see you soon," the nurse said. "In the meantime, enjoy breakfast . . . and no more cellular calls, all right?"

The nurse left Brennan to her meal and her thoughts.

The tray of food was nothing special—including oatmeal that looked about as appetizing as something off her worktable—but she ate it all, and was soon even wishing for a second cup of carburetor-fluid coffee.

Making sure there was no sign of the blond nurse in the corridor beyond her open door, Brennan got out her cell again, speed-dialed Booth, gave him a quick update, and suggested that he check his e-mail and print out the files Angela had sent him . . . and bring them along when he came to get her.

"Why," he asked, "are they releasing you again?"

"They never released me in the first place," she said.

"Good point. On my way."

An hour later, Booth walked through the door in his usual dark suit, conservative tie, and crisp white shirt.

Dr. Keller, on the other hand, had yet to make an appearance—"soon" being a relative term in any hospital—and Brennan wondered if the physician was punishing her for yesterday.

Booth, carrying two fat manila folders under an arm, plopped into the chair next to her bed.

"Well?" she asked.

He shook his head. "I haven't looked at 'em yet—didn't waste the time. Knew you'd want to see them, too."

"I like this new thoughtful side you're showing," she said, granting him a small smile. "I'll have to check into the hospital more often."

"Anyway, it's hard to read and drive at the same time."

Brennan took the file, surprised by its heft. "I didn't think Angela had this much. . . ."

"She didn't. When I saw that name *Battaglia*, I called over to the Chicago PD. They e-mailed me the files on both Battaglia and Parks, and I printed those out, too. Seems the Chicago PD has been transferring over their old files onto disk."

"Isn't science wonderful?" she said, and settled back on the bed, using the motor to raise her about forty-five degrees.

The name scribbled on the tab in Booth's handwriting was PARKS.

Not surprisingly, Booth had kept the mobster's file for himself, and was starting in on it as she read hers.

The information was discouragingly thin, albeit with wrinkles that Angela hadn't provided over the phone.

In 1948, David Parks had graduated from Northwestern as a certified public accountant, worked for a medium-sized company for two and a half years, then left under circumstances not outlined in the police report.

Four months later, Parks opened his own business in an office in the Silversmith Building at 10 South Wabash, which—for the eleven years prior to going missing—was his sole source of income.

The file indicated Parks had made a substantial living, at least by the standards of the nineteen fifties; but—after the investigation into his disappearance— the authorities began to suspect his practice may not have been entirely legitimate.

The missing person's report had been filed by one Terence Rhyne, who claimed that on the night of July 14, 1959, he had been scheduled to meet Parks at the Berghoff restaurant after work for drinks and dinner; but the accountant had not shown.

Known to be meticulously punctual, Parks had not phoned or messengered Rhyne, canceling their appointment (date?). Rhyne had grown worried and contacted the police. For the next six months, detectives searched for Parks with no success. Eventually, Parks went into the cold case file.

Brennan read and reread certain passages.

Around noon of the day of his disappearance, Parks had been seen at lunch in the Loop in the company of a man named Mark Koch, who also had an office in the Silversmith Building. A jeweler, Koch had lunch with Parks most days, and said that July fourteenth had been just like most every other shared luncheon with the accountant.

More witnesses, more statements . . . more of the same, and as Angela had suggested, everyone involved with the case indeed was male.

Unmarried, Parks had no noteworthy female acquaintances, not even sisters (he had none), and his mother was deceased.

The last page was Parks's client list, which was—as the police report noted—quite short.

Seven names . . .

. . . but one leapt at her.

Her eyes flashed to her partner, engrossed in the Battaglia file.

"Booth," she said.

Without looking up, he held up an index finger: he would be with her in what . . . a second, a minute, an hour?

This was one of the things about him that drove her mad. Whatever *he* was doing was always more important. . . .

Not this time.

"*Booth!*"

"What?" he said with a start.

A nurse leaned in. "Is everything all right?"

"Sorry," Brennan said sheepishly. "Didn't mean to yell."

The nurse cast her slitted-eyed disapproval, but said nothing and departed.

Brennan asked Booth, "You didn't look at these at all?"

"No," he said, one eye on the Battaglia file. "When I talked to Greene on the phone, he just said Parks was some accountant, and this goombah Battaglia mob muscle, not a real player."

"Well, the accountant?"

"Yeah?"

"He only had about a half dozen clients."

Booth shrugged. "And?"

"And one of them was named Anthony Gianelli."

Booth slammed closed the Battaglia file, rose and crossed to the bed in two steps. He snatched the thick file folder out of her hands.

"Help yourself," she said, folding her arms, an eyebrow arched.

"Thanks," he said, reading the file but not her sarcasm.

Dr. Keller came in, took in the FBI agent, whose nose was buried in the manila folder. "I suppose I shouldn't ask."

Ignoring Keller, Booth said, "This *has* to be the connection . . . but does it mean Jorgensen was somehow mobbed up? Tied to Gianelli?"

"Excuse me?" Dr. Keller asked. "I'm sure your case is important, Agent Booth. But so is mine, and her name is Brennan."

"Sorry," Booth said, shutting the folder.

Skirting the FBI agent, Dr. Keller asked, "Feeling better, Dr. Brennan?"

"Yes, thank you. A good night's sleep can do wonders."

"Often the best medicine," he said, and gave her a quick exam, cursory enough not to require Booth's absence, and pronounced her fit enough to check out.

"Good to hear, Doctor," she said.

The youthful physician half-smiled. "Really? Weren't you going to leave anyway?"

"Probably."

He sighed. "Well, I would hate to call security to restrain you, so let's just check you out. Your injuries are going to need time to heal, and I want you to take it easy."

"You can count on me, Doctor."

"Yes," Dr. Keller said, lifting both eyebrows, "but for what?"

Half an hour later—five minutes of which were devoted to Brennan refusing to ride in a wheelchair—she and Booth were in the hospital parking lot.

"We should go see Gianelli," Booth said, somehow managing to be glum and excited at once.

"Which one? Father or son?"

"Either. Both."

"With what for evidence?"

Booth kept walking, thinking, obviously trying to come up with an answer; but by the time they were seat-belted into the Crown Vic, he had still said nothing.

"Okay," he said finally, starting the car. "Maybe

you're right. We don't really have anything. We have to go *somewhere*."

"Yes, we do," Brennan said. "My hotel."

He pulled onto the ramp. "I'll bite—why?"

"I need my laptop."

"What's on your laptop?"

"Take me to my hotel and I'll show you."

He snorted a laugh. "A beautiful woman, a hotel room, and a suggestive remark—best offer I've had all day."

He headed toward the hotel.

"There was nothing suggestive about—"

"Joke," he said.

Including the "beautiful" part? she wondered.

Booth managed to keep his curiosity under wraps until they got to her hotel, but he was clearly anxious. They did not converse, however, and she could see he was chasing theories in his mind.

She did not give in to that pursuit—she preferred to have more data first.

He allowed her a quick shower and a change of clothes before sitting her down at the little desk with the hotel's high-speed Internet connection.

She pulled up the files that Angela had sent of the images she'd created with the Angelator, a program Angie developed that allowed rendering of 3-D holographic images based on measurements from the original skulls. With the Angelator, a face and hair could be given to what had been a bare skull.

Brennan turned the laptop to share the images with Booth, who had drawn a chair up beside her.

"This is making my brain hurt," Booth said.

"No comment," Brennan said.

"Parks was probably gay—"

"Possibly gay."

He gave her that. "Possibly gay, which made him a potential target for Jorgensen ... but Battaglia was the furthest thing from Jorgensen's victim profile."

"Can't a mob guy be gay?"

"Not one whose first arrest was a rape charge involving a sixteen-year-old waitress."

"Oh." She shifted her position. "And Parks had a connection to the Gianellis."

He nodded decisively. "*Both* these victims had a connection to the Gianellis."

They studied side-by-side pictures of the two men.

Battaglia had a wide, flat mug with the nose and big bulging eyes of a bulldog.

Parks was blond with blue eyes and angular, sharp features, including high cheekbones, adding up to a vague resemblance to an owl.

Her cell phone rang and she hit the button. "Brennan."

"Zach."

Her assistant Zach Addy—thin and bespectacled, with a mop of dark hair—was halfway through two doctorates, but looked more like he was halfway through his senior year in high school.

"What's up?" Brennan asked.

"Third skeleton just arrived, and we've started testing already. I thought you'd want to know."

"Thanks, Zach. Stay on it."

". . . Wait a minute, Jack wants to talk to you."

Hodgins got on the line. "Been looking more into the soil question."

"Hi, Jack. Soil question? Does it have an answer?"

"The sandy soil the first two skeletons were buried in is different than the soil under that Jorgensen guy's house."

"We knew that."

"Yes," Jack said, "but we know more now. I've been doing some further testing and comparisons, and the soil mixture from the skeletons matches a place called the Indiana Dunes Inland Marsh."

"Great work," Brennan said.

Jack said, "Thanks . . . just don't get too effusive. It's a smaller area to search than all of Chicago, but it's still several hundred acres."

"Where do we start?"

"I'd suggest the main gate."

". . . Thanks, Jack. It's a start. A good one."

"Yeah, and I got something off the third skeleton, too. Not sure what it is, but I've got it in the gas chromatograph/mass spectrometer now. I'll call ya back when I know what the substance is."

Brennan said, "Thanks," and ended the call.

She brought Booth up to speed on what she had

learned, and within minutes they were in the car headed for Indiana.

Booth had an Indiana map in the glove compartment and Brennan unfolded it as he drove.

"The Indiana Dunes?" Booth asked.

"Yes . . . What are you thinking?"

His eyes narrowed. "I'm thinking maybe it's the Dunes Express. . . ."

She had all but forgotten the odd expression Lisa Vitto had used, in relation to her missing boyfriend, that night at Siracusa.

In her defense, since then Brennan had suffered a mugging, numerous painkillers, and passing out at the Field Museum; but as soon as Booth spoke the words "Dunes Express," the case made sudden sense.

"A mob dumping ground," she said, "a burial ground for traitors and enemies."

"Where else do missing mob accountants and washed-up Outfit muscle wind up, after the lights go out?"

Her heart pounding, she said, "All right—what do we do?"

"How big is the area again?"

"According to Jack, several hundred acres."

He shook his head, jaw set. "Do we even *know* what we're searching for?"

"Graves, of course."

"But probably not with little headstones and white crosses marking them."

"Probably not."

"And the best part?" Booth said miserably. "It's in a swamp."

"Marsh, actually."

He barked a laugh. "Marsh, swamp, what difference does it make?"

"Swamp has a higher water table. If they were disposed of in a swamp, the bodies most likely would be hidden underwater instead of buried."

His eyes bored into her.

Hers bored back at him. "Would you please not stare at me when you're driving?"

He returned his gaze to the road. "What I was trying to say is . . . it's going to be hard."

"Unlike all the easy times we've had," she said.

That got a dry chuckle out of him.

"It *is* a big area," she allowed.

"It'll take a ton of agents to search the area, and most of them won't have any idea what they're looking for."

Brennan thought it over. "Narrow the field, and we could bring in ground-penetrating radar."

Around them, traffic slowed as they ran into Chicago's inevitable construction. Brennan watched out the window as they entered the Chicago Skyway, the scenery becoming more and more desolate.

The South Side had long been the neglected section of the city, made up predominantly of the working poor and those who were not even that lucky. As the road turned east toward Gary, the prospects did not improve.

The steel industry, which had once made Gary a thriving community, had for the most part turned to rust; and many of those left living here wore the faces of *Titanic* passengers as the water rose over the deck.

They might still be alive, but nothing was left to look forward to except death and release.

Brennan's phone chirped, obliviously good-natured, and she answered it to find Jack Hodgins on the other end again.

"What have you got, Jack?"

"That dust I told you about before?"

"Yeah?"

"It was on all the bones of the other two skeletons, too ... but in such small amounts I couldn't get a breakdown. This time? There was enough."

"You gonna keep me in suspense?"

"Sixty-four percent lime."

She hunched over, straining her seat belt. "Jorgensen's basement?"

"Whoa, whoa, whoa, Dr. Brennan. . . . Don't get ahead of yourself. Sixty-four percent lime, twenty-three percent silica, seven percent alumina, three percent each of iron oxide and sulfur trioxide."

Brennan took only a second to put the pieces together. "Cement."

"Cement."

"I thought you said the Indiana Dunes—where did the cement come from?"

Jack said, "My guess? A construction site or a demolition site. Whatever it is, it'll be in or near the Indiana Dunes Inland Marsh. And your bodies came from that patch of the Dunes."

They were off the expressway now, and Booth had turned east onto a two-lane highway, traffic finally moving again.

"Also," Jack said, "I've found traces of Typha, Cyperaceae, and Potamogetonaceae."

"Cattails, bulrushes, and pondweed," Brennan said. "That helps."

"The marsh is on Highway 12, south of the highway in Indiana."

"We're on our way there now," Brennan said. "You want me to paste the gold star on your chart, or can you handle it yourself?"

A grin was in his voice. "I'll wait for you, Doctor."

They rang off and she updated Booth as he drove.

"Where are we?" she asked.

"Highway 12."

She glanced around at a low-slung cityscape. On the North Side, railroad tracks ran parallel to them, woods beyond that, Lake Michigan beyond the woods. After a while a sign near the tracks said Chicago South Shore and South Bend Railroad.

She asked Booth, "How did you know to go this way?"

"I stashed Musetti down the road in a place called Ogden Dunes."

"As in Dunes Express?"

Booth looked pained.

"Sorry," she said.

"Truth hurts."

"You've been out here recently then, right?"

"Yeah."

"Was there any construction?"

He considered that. "They're renovating some of the homes along the lake."

"Are they using a lot of cement?"

"Not particularly, they're wood homes . . . but the Homeland Security Department is building a two-lane highway from the interstate to the south to U.S. Steel to the north."

"Homeland Security?" Brennan asked.

"Steel is considered intrinsic to national security. No steel, no tanks, no Humvees, no gun barrels. The HSD wants the road into the plant to be secure, so they're building it themselves."

"Where at?"

He pointed off to the left. "That over there?"

She could see the huge steel mill up the road a little north of the South Shore railroad tracks. "Yeah, U.S. Steel."

"Right," he said. "The road will come up to it from the right."

"Where's the marsh?"

"That's the west edge of it."

Brennan sat forward again. "They're building the road through the marsh?"

"Not quite, but close."

She stared at him.

"Don't go tree hugger on me now, Bones. Wasn't my idea to put the road there."

She stared harder.

"Hey, they're almost finished with it. Be done before winter. Seriously, I wouldn't have put it there either, but I wasn't consulted."

She didn't tell him that her reaction was not environmentalist in nature . . . at least, not entirely.

They passed the construction of the northbound highway, which was still a good half mile south of crossing Highway 12, and would have to bisect both 12 and the railroad tracks before it reached U.S. Steel.

She wondered why, if the HSD wanted the road secure, they would cross this highway and the tracks. This didn't make a lot of sense, but in her dealings with the FBI, she'd found that making sense did not seem to be high on the federal government's priority list.

She gave up trying to understand the government and watched the prevailing westerly wind carry dust past the car window.

Booth hit his right turn signal just as Brennan saw a sign for the Indiana Dunes Inland Marsh.

He pulled into the parking lot and turned again, stopping with the front bumper facing a log rail.

They alighted, and Brennan stretched.

It felt good to be out of the car. The dust wasn't so bad that you noticed it breathing, but she could see buildup on the leaves of nearby plants and the log in front of the car.

A huge framed map on log legs stood off to the right of the parking lot, the marshland trails plainly visible behind Plexiglas.

"What's next?" Brennan asked.

"We can't search it by ourselves," Booth said.

She shrugged and walked over to the map, Booth on her heels.

"When did this area become protected?" she asked.

"Why would you think I'd know that?"

Brennan got out her cell phone and speed-dialed.

"Zach Addy," her cell said.

"It's me."

"Dr. Brennan. And how are you?"

"Fine, Zach. Are you near your computer?"

"What do you think?"

"Are you online?"

"Of course."

She told him what she wanted to know, then listened to him tap some keys.

"The state park opened in 1926," he said.

"Are we in the state park?" Brennan asked Booth.

"Barely. This is the southeast corner of the Indiana

Dunes State Park; rest of it is across the road, runs back west from here."

"All right, Zach, thanks." She ended the call. "Okay, the park has been here since 1926. How long has the cement been here?"

"Maybe six months," Booth said, eyes tight.

Brennan studied the map and the winding trails that it showed. One trail led away from the parking lot, then—maybe a mile out—branched into different trails that serpentined around the marsh, all coming back to the main trail at that point.

"Depending on the wind," she said, "these trails are all too far from the construction to absorb a great deal of cement dust."

He frowned. "Are we in the wrong place?"

Back to the west, maybe a quarter of a mile, a smaller area (according to the map) had a modest parking lot, a few tables, and a single looping trail called the Inland Marsh Overlook.

This spot squatted in the shadow of the new highway.

She pointed at the map and grinned. "Booth, I think we just narrowed our search area. . . ."

They climbed back into the Crown Vic and he drove them to the picnic area. Westbound, a sign pointed to it; but looking up the highway, the sign they should have seen, coming from the west, had been sheared off and lay flat in the ditch next to the road.

No wonder they had missed it.

Booth pulled in and parked.

They got out again, this time Brennan more confident about their search. Booth popped the trunk and removed the trowel she'd used in Jorgensen's basement.

"You might want to lose the suit coat before we go," she said.

He took her advice, dropped it in the trunk, his gun looking even larger now without the jacket to hide it.

Picking up a folding shovel, he asked, "Do we need anything else?"

She shook her head. "Not yet. If we find something. . . . we'll deal with it then."

As they strode to the trail, she took the lead. It was his investigation, but this was her turf.

The sun was high in the autumn sky, a light breeze blowing from the west; although she wore a long-sleeved tee shirt, Brennan felt a slight chill and wished she'd brought a windbreaker.

Then again, a mile of walking through the woods would heat her up and she would probably end up wishing she'd worn a lighter-weight, short-sleeved shirt.

The trail was nothing more than a worn path through the high grass and foliage sprouting from the sandy soil. From the texture of the earth, Brennan knew they were much closer to finding the source of the skeletons than they ever had been in Jorgensen's basement.

A stray strand of hair tickled her face at the same time a stray thought tickled her mind. "Does Jorgensen have a valid driver's license?"

"I don't know. Why?"

"Well, if he's responsible for the skeletons, this is a long way from his house."

"Couple hours," Booth agreed.

"And if he had this place, why use his crawlspace?"

Booth frowned. "Do you still think he's the guy delivering skeletons, Bones?"

"That sounded a little redundant, don't you think? . . . I doubt Jorgensen's our skeleton assembler; but he's guilty of multiple homicides, which means you may wind up having to prove he *didn't* send them."

"To nail the right guy for this, you mean," he said, nodding. "Good point."

This sunny landscape was thick with pine and beech trees, leaves still on them, trees fooled by the drought and excessive heat that lasted beyond summer—not enough leaves to block out the sun, but trees and bushes were everywhere, as well as goldenrod and several other weedy-looking plants that Brennan didn't recognize.

She did recognize, however, that these were not the plants found in trace portions on the first two skeletons.

Brennan moved farther into the wilderness, her eyes scouring the ground for any clue, checking the plants for the level, if any, of cement dust accumulated on the leaves.

Finally, as they neared the marsh overlook—a green space with scattered picnic tables and trash cans—she started seeing cement dust on plant leaves.

Stopping, she pointed this out to Booth.

The FBI agent stepped forward, his face moist with sweat, rings starting under his arms. She could feel perspiration on her own face, her hair matted to her forehead, and figured she must be about as disheveled as he was.

"Cement dust," she said.

"So much for the marsh as wetlands," Booth said. "What did they do with the 'wet'?"

The ground they'd trod over hadn't seen rain in weeks or longer.

She sighed, hands on hips. "The drought's hit this area really hard. My guess, they're at least a foot short of normal rainfall."

Looking up ahead, she saw scraggly cattails and wispy bulrushes.

"Look sharp now," she told the FBI agent. "We're getting to where we should find something . . . *if* there's anything to be found."

"What exactly are we looking for?"

"Clues," she said.

He touched her shoulder and stopped her. "A little help, here, for the laymen in the crowd—what *kind* of clues?"

Facing him, she said, "You once told me that it was like pornography—I would know it when I saw it."

Clenching his jaw, he nodded.

Brennan put her head down and veered off the trail to the right, toward the construction site.

"Where are you going, Bones?" he asked, still on the pathway.

"If you were a killer," she said, without looking back at him, "would you bury the body on the trail?"

"I'd bury it in the marsh."

"Right."

Booth fell in behind her again.

Maybe a hundred yards off, on her left, something white winked at her from the ground near a clump of weeds.

She stopped . . .

. . . but it was gone.

Booth stopped too. "What?"

She said nothing, her eyes roving the area as if that alone would unearth whatever she had seen.

Nothing.

She backed up two steps, then saw it again. Keeping her eyes on the object, she moved to it and knelt. Dusty but white as a pearl in the sun, was a one-inch square buried in the dirt.

"What?" Booth repeated, next to her now, looking down.

"You don't see it?"

He squatted next to her, putting the thing in shadow. She used a hand to scoot him a foot to the left, letting the sun in again, and pointed to the white square.

"A rock?" he asked.

She looked at him. "A rock?"

"Not a rock?"

"How about a bone."

"You're sure?"

She tilted her head and arched both eyebrows at him.

He smiled weakly. "Of course you're sure. But is it human?"

"One way to find out. . . ."

She used her cell phone to snap three quick pictures from different distances, then eased the trowel in and met resistance.

Pulling the trowel out, she moved six inches farther from the square and tried again.

This time, no resistance.

She dug down, repeating the process all around the object until she had a perimeter.

Then she snapped more photos, before digging up as much ground as she could without disturbing the object.

With that done, she dug with the only tool she had more control of than the trowel—her hands.

The more she cleared, the more photos she took.

Unable to help, Booth walked a few steps away and made a cell-phone call.

When he finished, he said, "That was Woolfolk."

"What did he have to say?"

"Jorgensen's spilling his guts. He's talking so much

they can't shut him up. It's like a Dr. Phil show out of control."

"I don't know what—"

"Bones, he's been killing gay men for fifty years."

". . . That does fit the time frame of our made-to-order skeletons."

Booth was shaking his head. "Yeah, but he's denying that."

"He is?"

"And if he's done it, why would he? He's copped to over thirty murders, but Woolfolk says he vehemently denies delivering the skeletons."

"Oh?"

"Yeah—the guy who did that? Must have been sick, he says."

She went on digging. "Keep talking. Tell me more."

"Woolfolk says word on the street is that the other crime families are turning against the Gianellis."

She frowned and glanced at him, pausing in her work. "Turning on their own?"

"You've got to understand," Booth said. "The Gianellis run most everything, and what they don't run, they don't want. They're public figures . . . they're like rock stars or something. You remember John Gotti?"

She nodded.

"The older Gianelli's the same sort of gangster. He craves the attention, the crowds, and the younger Gi-

anelli is even worse. And ever since Al Capone attracted too much attention with the St. Valentine's
Day Massacre . . . you *have* heard of that?"

"Yes."

"Well, ever since, and particularly in modern times,
the mob has sought to be a low-profile operation."

She pulled the object free from the ground.
"There."

"Human?" Booth asked, moving closer.

Brennan held up a skull that was dirty but otherwise whole.

A human skull.

"Jackpot," Booth said.

"Could be," Brennan granted, "if we can match
dental records."

She swiveled the skull so Booth could see the back.
"And I'm thinking maybe *this* is the cause of death. . . ."

She pointed to where two small caliber bullets had
bored through the back of the skull.

"Double tap," Booth said. "Mob-style execution."

"We're going to need more people," Brennan said,
"and ground-penetrating radar."

"You have but to ask," Booth said, getting out his
cell phone. "I think we just found ourselves a Mafia
graveyard."

"Whatever it is," she said, "this is most likely the
source of our skeletons . . . and there are probably
more."

Booth called for help and then, as he was putting

the cell away, his eyes panned toward the construction site and froze.

Then he was smiling, his eyes wide.

"What?"

"*That's* why," he said. "The construction's coming too close to the graveyard! They had to move it. They couldn't risk us finding all these bodies!"

"Possible," she allowed, not wanting to go much further without proof.

"It's logical, Bones. Just the kind of thing you like. The mob's been burying guys out here for God only knows how long, and now with the drought exposing their hiding place, and the encroaching construction? They had to move the bodies. More than that, get rid of them. . . . Then, to throw us off the track, they put us on the trail of a serial killer."

"How would they even *know* about that?" she asked skeptically.

"Trust me, no one knows what goes on in their city better than the Outfit." He waved his arms. "The cops, us feds, we're just trying to keep our heads above water; but the mob guys? They know every-thing, *anything* that might help them turn a buck."

"There's a certain logic to what you say," she ad-mitted.

"Thank you."

"But how does knowing about a madman like Jor-gensen help them 'turn a buck'?"

He frowned, just a little.

"Don't mean to rain on your parade," she said.

"No. Valid point. Gotta think about that, Bones. . . . Don't let me stop you."

If they were standing in the middle of a graveyard, she was going to be busy for a very long time.

She surveyed her surroundings.

This was a big area to search. Would be more like one of those mass graves in Bosnia or Guatemala.

Booth was on his phone again, this time relaying news of their find to the higher-ups while Brennan poked around the ground, wondering how many sorry souls had taken the one-way ride on the Dunes Express.

Knowing that, dead gangsters or not, they deserved the dignity of identification.

10

THE INLAND MARSH SITE SWARMED WITH AGENTS, cops, and crime scene techs.

Not only had Booth and Brennan narrowed the focus of their search, a combination of science, drought, and luck had helped them win the forensics lottery: actually finding a skull.

Already the Chicago PD was going through missing persons records, trying to get a dental match with Brennan's discovery, while the same information had been forwarded to the FBI computers.

The skull itself would be sent to Brennan's staff at the Jeffersonian for them to add their insights and expertise.

Right now Brennan was supervising a pair of techs operating the ground-penetrating radar. To their right, a Chicago PD Crime Scene Unit was literally dug in, doing exploratory work in spots flagged as potential graves.

Other FBI agents had searched the area and found signs that the park had been home to considerable digging, particularly the ground nearer the construction site; still other agents were searching farther down the trail in either direction.

Several agents were at the Visitor's Center and ranger station, questioning anyone they could find. Still other FBI personnel, down at the Dirksen Building, had started delving into any mob-related crimes that might have a victim who ended up here. (That would be a long list.)

For his own part, Seeley Booth had been thinking.

Seemingly unconnected pieces—pieces from what he'd thought were separate puzzles—were fitting together; he was seeing things from a different angle. Now he could flip the situation one hundred eighty degrees and examine it from the bad guy's point of view.

This was obviously mob-related: dead Outfit members made up at least part of the two wired-together skeletons, and now a double-tapped skull in sandy soil tied to those skels. Coincidences didn't come that big, and Booth—like most law enforcement officers—didn't believe in *small* coincidences. . . .

The mob had been burying bodies out here for years, the Dunes Express; that much seemed indisputable.

So, why move them?

The road construction was the obvious answer, plus the drought bringing deep buried bodies near the surface, both fueling the worry that if one body might be discovered, so would more.

And if the authorities ever got an idea of how many one-way rides had been taken out here, well, there'd be hell to pay. Better to move 'em out.

But then what to do with them?

Maybe somebody had got a bright idea.

Somebody who (for whatever reason) knew the pattern of certain local killings, and knew as well who the prime suspect was for those killings—a literally *old* suspect just waiting to take the fall.

If skeletons seemed to start coming from a serial killer, as a last thumbing-of-the-nose at the cops he'd eluded all these years, whoever would think the Outfit was implicated?

Besides, what could the FBI make out of a pile of mismatched bones?

Plenty, Booth thought, watching the activity around him, *plenty*.

His eyes found Brennan hard at work with the radar boys, and he smiled. The "mastermind" behind all this had not counted on Booth's secret weapon: Temperance Brennan.

On having determined the makeshift graveyard to be mob-related. Two alternatives presented themselves. One, the Gianellis, the main crime family in

Chicago, were behind the skeleton scam; or two, someone in the rival families was trying to frame them for it, in a power play designed in part to rid the town of these Gotti-like self-styled superstar mobsters who had attracted so much unwanted federal heat.

Booth approached Brennan as she sat on a folding chair watching a laptop computer monitor on a small portable table near where the techs worked the ground-penetrating radar.

"Doesn't look like anything's there," she said to the tech. "Try another two feet north."

"Got a minute?" Booth asked.

She lifted her face from the monitor. "In a job that takes hours, there's always a minute."

"You okay?"

Her eyes were bright, but the circles under them were dark.

"Never better."

"Bones, if you pass out on me again—"

"Why don't we agree never to mention that? . . . You're on your own for a while, Ernie."

The tech nodded and resumed his search.

Brennan followed Booth and the two of them found a private place on the periphery.

He told her his theory.

"This isn't my field," she said.

"No, but it's your case, and you spent time with Gianelli. I trust your instincts. I trust your mind."

"You think it really could be a rival mob family?"

He shrugged. "Lot of people in Chicago don't like the Gianellis. Find them an embarrassment. Plus, there's money to be made by taking over their—"

Her cell phone rang. "Brennan."

Booth watched as she listened.

Brennan's face grew surprised, then amazed.

"You have *got* to be *kidding* me," she said.

Her eyes locked with Booth's as she listened some more, then ended the call with, "Thanks, Jack. You're tops."

Putting the phone back on her belt, she said, "That was Jack."

Booth nodded. "I'm a detective. I deduced that."

"We've got a DNA match on the clavicle from the latest skeleton—one of the bones that had never been buried."

"I remember. That's why you looked surprised?"

An eyebrow arched. "Not surprised they got a match . . . just who the bone turned out to belong to."

"So who, already?"

"I'm not sure if you'll view this as good news or bad news, Booth. But it's your witness—the DNA match is Stewart Musetti."

Booth took the news like a physical blow. "You're sure," he said.

It wasn't exactly a question.

She was nodding. "You took his DNA when he entered the Federal Witness Protection Program, just in case anything like this ever happened, right?"

He nodded back numbly.

"I know you didn't want to lose this witness," she said. "But you knew he was probably dead. His girlfriend said he'd taken the Dunes Express, and we're at the last stop right now."

"Oh yeah."

"So you've answered your own question, Booth. It's not a rival gang."

He was recovering fast. "That means the *Gianellis* are behind all of this."

She was thinking. "Booth, I don't mean to overstep . . ."

"Overstep, overstep!"

"Could *I* . . . float a theory?"

"Float away."

She touched a finger to the side of her chin. "Suppose the younger Gianelli—Vincent—got the assignment from his father to get rid of these bones. We've already found evidence of areas surrounding us that show signs of digging. So the corpse removal is a gradual project."

"As the construction nears," Booth said, getting it, "they clear more gravesites."

"Right. Perhaps they bring in a truck, a dump truck possibly, and just rudely toss their excavated findings into the back of it, the skeletons coming apart until a literal pile of bones remains."

Booth nodded again. "They wouldn't exactly stand on ceremony."

"So," she continued, "we can presume Vincent did any number of things with the unearthed skeletons . . . dumped them in the lake, buried them elsewhere, perhaps ground them up at a butcher shop associated with his restaurant . . ."

"You're scaring me," he told her, but was smiling. "That's good. That's all well reasoned."

"You don't have to sound surprised. But somewhere along the line 'mastermind' Vincent has an idea. A surprisingly complex one. He will use some of these bones to simultaneously taunt the FBI *and* distract them from the Musetti disappearance—with luck, even getting Seeley Booth pulled off the Musetti case."

His eyes narrowed. "Well, it's true that the skel showing up on our doorstep made it a federal matter—if it hadn't turned up on Uncle Sam's property, it would've been strictly Chicago PD's affair. But how could Vincent assume I'd be pulled off the case?"

"Booth, I talked to the man. He claims to be a fan, and without a doubt he knows about me, knows that you and I've worked a number of cases together involving my specific anthropological skills."

"I don't know. Now this is seeming thin. . . . Is that slick idiot capable of—"

"He's not an idiot, Booth. He is slick, all right. And cunning. And you know what else? He may or may not be a Temperance Brennan fan, but he is sure as hell a serial killer buff."

Booth frowned. "Really? How do you know this?"

"Ever eat at Siracusa? I have."

"I know you have. Actually, I don't exactly hang out there."

"He has a 'Wall of Fame'—framed photos?"

Booth was nodding. "Typical celebrity display, sure. Lots of restaurants do that, particularly the Italian ones."

"Do they 'typically' include shots of the owner smiling and shaking hands with John Wayne Gacy?"

"You're kidding."

"I wish. He bragged to me about his interest in crime and mystery and in particular serial killers. He would be in a perfect position to know all about the prime suspect in those gay young men disappearances . . . a big-fish suspect who got away."

"So," Booth said, "he puts us on Jorgensen's trail. Distracts us and laughs at us . . ."

She held up a palm. "It's just a theory, remember. The evidence gathering has just begun. . . ."

"Right, and I think I know how to get some evidence on Vincent, and digging in the ground won't be how I do it."

"How, then?"

"Bones, does Vincent Gianelli strike you as the kind of guy who could build a skeleton from scratch, with the schooling he's had?"

She thought about it. "Probably not. I said he wasn't dumb, and that he was slick and cunning. But smart? Well educated? No."

"Exactly," Booth said. "Maybe while his pals were grinding up bones or chugging out into the middle of Lake Michigan for dropping off chums for chum, Vince kicked back and did some reading."

Her forehead tightened. "How does that get you more evidence?"

Booth grinned. "It doesn't. But the Patriot Act, Section 215, does."

"Which is what?"

"The section that allows a Special Agent like me to find out what our suspect has been reading."

Her mouth dropped. Horror-struck, she said, "You're *not*."

"Sure I am. Why wouldn't I?"

"It's an invasion of privacy! You're taking a case that is one part evidence, one part circumstance, and another part theory, and using that as a pretext to invade Vincent Gianelli's privacy."

"Yeah, and who cares? It's legal."

Her eyes blazed. "That doesn't make it right."

"Why do you even care? This is my part of the job, not yours."

"One, I'm a writer. Two, I'm a citizen of the United States, and all citizens should be outraged by this kind of—"

Booth snorted. "What, Bones? Afraid I'll find out he's been reading your book? Or maybe the competition?"

She glared at him for a long moment. Then, calm

but having to work at it, she said, "Booth—I have been to Bosnia, Guatemala, Thailand, and half a dozen other places where one group of people tried to enslave or eradicate another."

"I know," Booth said, his tone respectful. He had been to some of those places, too—with a gun.

She was asking, "Do you know what the aggressor group had in common in each case?"

Booth shook his head.

"*Control.* They all tried to control the other group by controlling information."

He held up his hands in surrender. "Look, I'll concede your point; I don't disagree with your politics. But this is the law of the land right now, and I'm law enforcement. Anyway, I don't want to 'control' Gianelli. If he's got nothing to hide, then he's got nothing to fear."

She stabbed the air with a finger. "You just don't get it, do you? You sound like the Nazis in 1937, the McCarthyites in 1953, the—"

"Nazi?" he exploded. "Now you're calling me a Nazi? Well, that's the limit!"

He stormed away, leaving her and her self-righteous beliefs behind, and when she called out, "Booth!" he ignored it.

He had work to do.

Woolfolk had showed up a while ago, and Booth assigned him to supervise the site while he went back into the city to get the necessary paperwork.

Then Booth approached two chain bookstores and the local library nearest Vincent Gianelli's home.

Whether due to what Brennan had said, or because as he performed this search he actually had time to think about it, he did feel a little dirty about these tactics, legal or not. He had performed police work for years now, and this felt a lot like something else.

That didn't stop him from utilizing the results.

The library list showed that Vincent Gianelli had not visited any library in the greater Chicago area since he was a sophomore in high school. (Booth was not the least bit surprised.)

But the Barnes & Noble list showed the purchase of half a dozen serial killer books, and two or three on anatomy; and Borders had their customer special-ordering a tome about the skeletal system.

This moment of glory was not all he'd hoped it would be—instead, he felt a little empty.

But he did have the information he needed to feel confident that Vincent Gianelli was the "mastermind" behind the assembled skeletons.

A knock on the jamb of his open office door got Booth's attention.

Brennan stood there.

"Mind if I . . . ?"

"Come in. Please. Make yourself comfortable."

She wore jeans, a white blouse, and a loose gray jacket, hair tied back in a ponytail; she appeared herself, rested and attractive, and certainly healthier than she had since being attacked in that hotel parking ramp.

Twenty-four hours had passed since their spat at the Inland Marsh, and they hadn't spoken since Booth had stomped off yesterday.

Now, with her sitting across from him, the tense silence hung between them, an invisible curtain.

She said, "Doing all right?"

He shrugged. "Fine."

She looked at the floor. "I, uh . . . guess I probably owe you an apology."

"Really?"

"Nazi was probably a little . . . strong."

"You think?"

"I should have probably settled for fascist."

He blinked.

But she was smiling.

She said, "I really am sorry."

He tossed the pencil he'd been using onto the desk, sighed, and leaned back. "You know, I'm sorry, too. I'm not big on this ends-justifies-the-means crap, even when the law permits it."

"But, uh . . . you went through with it, right?"

"Yeah. I'm afraid I didn't feel regret till after I'd done the deed."

"Hard to feel regret before," she said with a shrug.

He held up the sheaf of papers. "Right here—purchases of serial killer books, anatomy, skeletal system. . . ."

"Do you still think that was the only way to get to Vincent?"

Booth considered that. "All I could think of."

She nodded and pulled a small plastic bag from her pocket.

"What's that?" he asked.

"You remember the hair I got from the wire knot on the third skeleton, the one at the cemetery?"

"Yeah—is it human?"

"Actually, no."

He let out another sigh, heaving this one. "I should have known it'd come to nothing . . . just like so much else in this case."

"It's canine," Brennan said.

He frowned at her curiously. "Dog hair?"

"Not just *any* dog—a Neapolitan mastiff." She gave him an innocent smile that was guilty as hell. "Anybody you know own one of those?"

". . . Vincent Gianelli."

"Right. And I didn't have to invade his privacy to get it."

"Is it from his dog?"

She shrugged. "Well, we won't know until we test it; but it's a rare enough breed that it should constitute probable cause."

Booth thought about saying something, talked himself out of it, and instead said, "I'm going to go see him."

"Good idea."

"Want to . . . come with?"

She grinned. "Thought you'd never ask. . . ."

Though the father divided his time between a Gold Coast apartment and a Forest Park mansion, Vincent Gianelli lived in Des Plaines, in a rambling two-story palace on a secluded estate at the very end of Big Bend Lane.

Booth and Brennan did not arrive alone.

Woolfolk was on hand, along with Chicago Police Lieutenant Greene (technically an observer), and an FBI SWAT team.

A wrought-iron gate blocked the driveway, but when Booth announced them through the squawk box, no response followed.

"Guy could be in there destroying evidence," Booth said to Brennan in the passenger seat.

Booth got on his walkie-talkie and gave the order.

Within a minute, the SWAT team had blown the gate.

SWAT went through first, some on foot, some riding in their truck. Booth and Brennan followed in the Crown Vic, Woolfolk and Greene in another car behind them.

They sped up the curving, wooded lane toward the front of the house while the SWAT team moved through the woods, searching for Vincent's security staff. After parking behind the SWAT truck, Booth got out, walkie in hand, Brennan on his heels.

The house was brick and about a block long, main entrance tucked into a portico in the center on the west side. Four double windows on either side of the entrance mirrored those one floor above. A wide chimney took up part of the front, matching others on each of the three exterior walls.

Booth had studied a layout of the estate and knew a huge garage and workshop were out back, as well as a guesthouse and a small bungalow for guards and other employees.

A voice came over the radio. "Woods clear."

A SWAT guy rang the bell and, when nothing happened immediately, a crash bar smashed into the knob and the door swung open and careened off the wall, then limply swung back, hanging loose like a broken tree limb.

The SWAT guys fanned out through the house.

More "clear" calls started coming almost immediately.

The house was empty.

Not even Gianelli's dog seemed at home.

Booth led the way to the back. While SWAT checked the guesthouse and bungalow, Booth, Brennan, Woolfolk, and Greene took the garage.

Booth shot off the lock and they entered, Booth in the lead.

The room was dark and Booth hit the light switch by the door.

The cars and SUVs behind the four overhead doors were two deep, making eight that they had to search on their way through the big room to the single door at the far end: Bentley, Hummer, Porsche, Escalade, Jaguar, Aston Martin, Ferrari, and Vincent's favorite, a '63 Corvette.

Taking a deep breath and letting it out, Booth twisted the knob and swung through the door crouching, his gun leveled.

He found a large machine shop, tools, workbenches, and heavy machinery scattered around . . .

. . . but no Gianelli.

The "all clear's" came in from the bungalow and guesthouse.

Booth frowned, the gun grip cold in his hand.

What, had aliens snatched them all?

From sarcasm he shifted to cold reality: had they been tipped off? Maybe by the same insider who had tipped the Gianellis about where to find Stewart Musetti?

If so, the tipster had to be FBI and, sooner or later, Booth would trap that rat.

Brennan found the next door, behind a large lathe in the corner. She stepped aside to let Booth take the lead.

The door opened onto a dark room, a spiral staircase going down into darkness. Using a mini-flash, Booth found a light switch and flipped it, bathing the room below in fluorescent light.

Instantly Booth recognized the workroom of a madman.

In the chamber below were worktables, not unlike the ones at the Field Museum. A headless skeleton lay on the one nearest the stairs, blood on the table and floor around it.

Brennan moved around him to survey the remains from up close. Booth descended the stairs, his eyes on the scientist, her eyes on the blood.

She followed it, looking at the floor beyond the table, and said, "Oh, no. . . . Sad. How sad. . . ."

Booth sped up now, coming around the table and pointing his gun down . . .

. . . but what he saw made him holster his weapon.

On the floor in a pool of blackened blood lay Gianelli's dog, its throat cut.

In a huge tub along one wall resided evidence of a hydrogen peroxide bath, a tag stuck between the toes of the headless skeleton.

Brennan picked it up and unfolded the printed-out note, which read:

POP THE TRUNK.

They trooped back upstairs, Booth making a beeline for Vincent's Vette. The keys were in the lid and he indeed popped the trunk, and found exactly what he expected to find.

The head of Vincent Gianelli.

This had little impact on Brennan, who had seen more than her share of severed skulls, even if she had not long ago spoken to this one firsthand. This skull still had much of its flesh, muscle, and hair.

Vincent's face possessed a strangely peaceful cast, belied by the hematomas on his cheeks and ragged neck, which told the anthropologist that the defleshing of the younger Gianelli's bones had at least started while he was still alive.

Not a pleasant way to leave the planet.

The others all backed up when Brennan used her cell phone to snap a photo of the head, then with a latex-gloved hand promptly pulled it out of the trunk by its hair and tipped it so she was looking up Vincent's neck from the bottom.

She wanted to see where it had been severed.

Replacing the head in the trunk, Brennan trudged back downstairs to count cervical vertebrae. She was sure that the number left with the skull and those on the skeleton would add up to seven.

She was right.

Though they would do more testing, this skeleton obviously belonged to one person: their deceased host.

She wheeled to find Booth standing behind her. "Who do you suppose did this?"

He shook his head.

"Will you investigate this one?"

"Yeah. But mob killings are rarely solved and prosecuted. These are pros."

Her eyes went from the skeleton to the dog, and she asked, "Who could do a thing like this?"

"Whoever was ordered to," Booth said coolly. "All about business with these people."

"Horrible business," she said with a small shudder.

Carefully, Booth put an arm around her. "That's why we go after them so hard." He gave her a little squeeze, then released her.

She could hardly believe he had done that. She had no idea what to say.

Booth's expression was grave. "I need to tell his father. Raymond Gianelli. You can come with if you want."

". . . Should I?"

Shrugging, he said, "Your call. But you *were* the one to identify the body."

He had a point.

11

To Temperance Brennan, Raymond Gianelli's monstrous home made his son's mansion look like a guesthouse.

Tucked away in a quiet Forest Park neighborhood, only the high wall around the property gave a hint at the nature of the man's business. Within the grounds, however, armed guards patrolled with attack dogs and—unlike at Vincent's place—everybody here was still on duty.

At the gate, two burly guys in black jumpsuits glared at Booth and Brennan, but inspected their IDs and let them pass.

Booth drove up a short drive to the front, where two more gunmen in black jumpsuits waited, looking like bad-guy SWAT team members.

The FBI agent and the anthropologist were escorted into a mahogany-paneled office off the entranceway. A desk bigger than three of hers dominated the room, a huge leather chair behind. Two chairs waited on this side of the desk, and Brennan had the same feeling she got in middle school when called to the principal's office.

Raymond Gianelli strode in, his dark, well-tailored suit immaculate, his face a blank mask as he took his place in the big chair, without shaking hands. "What *now*, Special Agent Booth?"

Booth's face was serious, no animosity in his eyes at all as he said, "I don't relish this task, Mr. Gianelli, despite our adversarial relationship. . . . We're here to inform you that your son Vincent has been murdered."

Gianelli didn't move, his expression didn't change. ". . . How?"

Brennan opened her mouth, but before she could utter a sound, Booth put a hand on her arm.

She clammed up.

Booth said, "Does it matter?"

The gangster's chin dropped to his chest and he rubbed his forehead. "You know it does. It's not like you to pull punches, Agent Booth."

Booth hesitated, and Gianelli, straightening up, demanded, "How did my son *die*?"

Brennan spoke, her voice low, professional. "He was tortured—we don't know how long as yet—and his head was severed. He was alive at the time. I'm sorry."

Booth was frowning, perhaps even irritated, but Gianelli only nodded and said, "Thank you."

To Booth, the gang boss asked, "Who is she?"

"Dr. Brennan is an anthropologist who sometimes works with—"

"You could stand to learn from her," Gianelli interrupted. His voice was strong but, if you listened carefully, a tremor could be detected. "She has a nice way with the truth."

"She does," Booth admitted.

"Where is my boy now? I want to see him."

"No, sir," Brennan said. "You don't."

Gianelli stared at her, his eyes dark marbles, his face a mask of pain and anger. "I want to see *him* for *myself.*"

"It's your right," Booth said.

Raymond Gianelli rode with them, no bodyguards, no gunmen, no lawyer, just the three of them.

They drove to the Cook County morgue, to which Vincent's remains had been transferred.

In the basement, in a cold, green hallway with one bench and two windows at the corridor's end, they waited.

Soon they were standing on either side of the father, facing a window behind which a blank-faced worker in hospital greens rolled in a sheet-covered cart.

Brennan wondered if Gianelli noticed the abnormally large lump where the head was. While the rest of the body lay flat, the head stood upright and the sheet rose a good six inches more than normal.

With the cart next to the window, the worker on the other side withdrew the sheet to reveal Vincent's head.

A hand shot to Raymond Gianelli's mouth and a horrified murmur escaped his lips. Surely Gianelli had seen almost everything in his long and illegal life; but this was too much, even for him.

The sheet was drawn a little farther back, and Brennan followed Gianelli's eyes to the skeleton.

Then his eyes closed, tears fell, and Raymond Gianelli—who had mercilessly murdered and ordered God only knew *how* many more—wobbled as though he might drop.

Automatically, Brennan and Booth each grabbed an arm and steered him away from the window to the long, wooden bench. He sagged and sat, weeping shamelessly.

Softly Booth said, "We are sorry for your loss."

Gianelli glared up at the FBI agent. "*Really?* Tell the truth like your lady friend here—don't you *love* that my son is dead, and there's one less Gianelli in the world?"

Booth kept his voice even. "No parent should have to bury a child."

Brennan could tell that Gianelli was eager for a fight, perhaps intent on picking one so rage could blot out sorrow; but Booth's words, his obvious sincerity, stopped the man cold.

His face fell into his hands.

They drove him home in silence, Gianelli in the back, lost in his thoughts, Brennan thinking about how everything up until now seemed like a warm-up for the Old School gangster bloodbath that would surely follow.

As they turned into Gianelli's driveway, he said, "I want to make a deal."

Booth shook his head. "All due respect to your situation, Mr. Gianelli, nothing has changed. I told you before, sir, no more deals. I offered you one in the deposition room, and you turned it down."

Brennan could hardly believe what she was hearing, and started to speak, but Booth's eyes shut her down.

He was up to something.

She swiveled slightly to see Gianelli in the backseat. He rubbed his forehead wearily.

"I'll tell you all of it, anyway," he said. "Not just our family, but the others. I know everything everyone's ever done in this town."

"You can't fight them all," Booth said. "You want to use me as your weapon of revenge. I'm not playing."

Gianelli's eyes and nostrils flared. "You think this is a fucking game, you FBI prick?"

Booth said nothing.

They were parked in front of Gianelli's house; one of Gianelli's men had a hand on the vehicle's rear door, but something had kept the guard from opening it. A gesture or look from Gianelli had maintained their privacy.

Whatever it had been, Brennan missed it.

Finally Booth spoke: "I'm the only way you have to get at the others now. Agreed?"

"... Agreed."

"Problem for you, Mr. Gianelli, is I can put them away now *without* your help. And put you away, too, no deals. . . . Unless, of course, you have something to trade that hasn't occurred to me. Otherwise, we have nothing more to talk about."

Gianelli sat for a long time without saying anything. When he did, his voice was soft and Brennan had to strain to hear.

"I know what you want, Booth."

"Do you?"

"You want the guy who gave us Musetti. You want the rat."

"I'm listening."

Gianelli hunched over. "I give you that guy, we'll cut a deal?"

Still facing front, Booth said, "You'll get hard time, Raymond, but we'll protect you. White-collar country club with no other mob guys. Nobody to cut you in the shower, unless it's a fallen congressman or Enron exec needing a buck."

"You're funny."

"Give me the federal leak, and we *will* take the others out. Those responsible for the atrocity perpetrated upon your son will go down. Give us enough, we'll bust them down to the root."

Gianelli's sigh had gravel and regret in it. "Hardest thing I ever did, havin' Stewie whacked. Musetti and me, we grew up together, our papas were pals, we were best buddies, compadres. Woulda been for our whole lives, too, only somebody started talkin' to him, fillin' his head with shit that we was gonna whack him. Which was bull—I *loved* that guy. But he threatened my family . . . threatened Vincent. And my boy wasn't perfect, but I loved him. And I couldn't allow that."

"I understand," Booth said.

"Finally, when we couldn't convince Stewie we weren't after his ass, I had to have Stewie taken out . . . to save my son. And the son of a bitch, the very bastard who filled Stewie with all that nonsense about us wanting him gone? Well, he's the very same bastard who sold him out to us. I will give him to you gladly, Agent Booth."

Brennan's eyes were on Booth now. His breathing seemed rapid and shallow, but he said nothing, sitting, staring through the windshield, not even looking in the rearview.

At last Gianelli said, "Special Agent in Charge Robert Dillon."

Booth nodded, as if this were old news.

Brennan, however, almost fell off the seat.

Dillon?

She eyed Booth—was he believing this? Where was the proof?

As if in reply to her thoughts, Gianelli said, "I have evidence for you in a safe-deposit box—audiotapes of the bastard that he don't know about. You want them?"

"Yes." Booth turned to look at the man he'd been talking to. "I'll have a man accompany you to the bank, Mr. Gianelli, to collect that evidence. You go on in and I'll arrange that."

Gianelli nodded.

Booth said, "Let me clear the rat out of our nest, and then we'll meet you back here."

Gianelli made a slight gesture with his hand, his man opened the door and he climbed out, no wobble in his step now.

As the elder statesman of organized crime headed into his mansion, Booth and Brennan rolled slowly away from and back around the circular drive.

"You believe him?" she asked.

Booth glanced at her. "What's his motivation to lie?"

"He's a liar. With a dead son to avenge."

"The latter is true, Bones, but the former? Gianelli is a lot of things, but a liar isn't one of them. Within his world, he plays by the rules. His word is gold. Matter of honor."

"Then you do believe him?"

"Hard not to. Despite everything he's done over the years, Gianelli is on the federal side now."

She frowned. "That's hard to picture."

"Do you think his enemies will be satisfied with just killing Vincent?"

"Oh. Well, no. Of course not."

"Raymond's motives are twofold. As you said, he wants revenge."

They were moving in slow traffic now, headed back to Booth's office.

Booth continued: "What I didn't say, directly, was that he needs protection. If his rivals hit Vincent, they can get to him. He and I both knew that, but there was no reason to say it."

"Shield his manhood from embarrassment in front of a female, huh?"

Booth nodded. "Gianelli's Old World, in his way."

"And Dillon? Did you suspect him before?"

"Actually . . . yeah."

"And you never *mentioned* it?"

He grinned at her, a very boyish grin, she thought.

"Bones, I had nothing but a hunch. No evidence, no data at all. I'm gonna share that with a scientist? No way."

She sat back, somewhat overwhelmed by the events of the day.

In the meantime, Booth called Special Agent Woolfolk and told him what was going on. Apparently

Booth had shared his suspicions with his other partner, because the explanation did not take long.

By the time they got to the office, Woolfolk had started tracking the money, and in under two hours—after a phone call from the bank, confirming the existence and the content of the audiotapes in Gianelli's safe-deposit box—they had enough on Dillon to go forward.

Brennan followed the two agents into Dillon's office.

The square-jawed, eagle-beaked SAC sat behind a desk nominally smaller than Gianelli's. He wore a well-tailored dark suit, a white-and-blue striped shirt with a white collar, and a yellow tie.

"News on the marsh dig?" he asked.

Booth said, "You have the right to remain silent . . ."

"*What?*"

"Do you understand your rights, Robert?"

"Of course I do! Explain yourself, Booth!"

"Raymond Gianelli gave you up, Robert. Seems he's resentful of his business rivals after they cut off his kid's head and stripped him into a skeleton, and he wanted to make a friend in the FBI. So he gave me . . . you."

"And you believe that lying mobster son of a bitch?" Dillon roared, rising, his hands open-palmed and shaking in indignation.

Woolfolk waved a manila folder. "We tracked the money, Robert."

Booth said, "And then there are the audiotapes."

"*What* audiotapes?"

Booth's smile was nasty. "Ah, I don't wanna ruin it for you. You'll find out soon enough."

"Goddamn it! This is a frame! I've been after those goombahs for years, and this is their payback."

"Payback," Booth said. "Good word. Sit down, Robert. Maybe I will tell you about it. . . ."

Booth laid it all out and, gradually, Dillon's anger subsided and he sagged back into the chair, as if trying to disappear into it.

Booth's voice held no humor as he said, "Let's put it this way, Bob—a hard rain's gonna fall."

Dillon just sneered at Booth.

Brennan felt like she had missed something. Hard rain? What was that about?

"That's why the abductors didn't whack our four agents, isn't it?" Booth asked. "That was part of the deal. You're *that* loyal to the Bureau."

"Go to hell, Booth."

"Care to tell us why you did it? Was it just the money?"

From that point on, Dillon decided to assert his right to remain silent, even as Woolfolk cuffed him and led him out through the office.

As for Temperance Brennan, she had a lab to run, an eight-hundred-year-old Native American to get back to. . . .

But her plane wasn't scheduled to depart until the

next morning, so, as the sun set, she accompanied Booth back to Gianelli's home in Forest Park.

"You really think he'll be here?" she asked as they parked.

"He's got nowhere else to go. Plus we're watching the place."

"Ah."

"Still, the contract on Raymond Gianelli will be worldwide. If he ran to Tibet and climbed to the top of Everest, they would still find him and kill him."

She said, "Easiest route up Everest is from the south, through Nepal."

"Really," Booth said. "Good to know."

As Booth had surmised, Gianelli was waiting for them in his office. He wore a button-down black shirt, open at the collar, and black slacks. He might have been ten years older than this morning.

The old mobster turned away and stared out the only window in the room, gazing somewhere off into the darkening woods.

"You ready to go?" Booth asked.

"You took care of your problem?"

"Dillon's in custody."

"Then I'm ready to go."

He stood silently for a long moment, then turned to face them, his cheeks wet with tears. "I didn't like his idea about the skeletons. I thought it was excessive. Too far out there, y'know? But I tried to respect his ideas, so he could stand on his own feet, outa my shadow. Said he thought that if you was looking for a serial killer? You'd leave us alone."

"And it helped," Booth said, "that my boss Dillon took me off Musetti and assigned me to that case."

"I guess it did. Maybe the kid knew what he was doing, after all."

"How did Vincent even *know* about Jorgensen?"

Gianelli gave a sad smile. "Booth, nobody farts in this town unless we know about it. Guy was killing fags, why should we give a shit? Public service far as we was concerned. And Vincent, he was interested in true crime. Serial killers, them sicko creeps. Why, I'll never know."

Brennan cringed at the word "fag." Like many in his world, Gianelli was a practicing Roman Catholic who considered homosexuality a sin, and many of Gianelli's generation and social strata considered it repugnant.

The hypocrisy underlying that gave Brennan a flash of understanding.

Even though Raymond Gianelli loved his son, as any father might love his son, the man cared nothing about human life in general.

She had thought Vincent a sociopath, which no doubt he was; but he'd come by it honestly, heredity and environment teaming to provide his lack of conscience.

The streets, the world, would be safer with these two gone.

She knew Booth would make Gianelli live up to his end of the bargain, which meant dozens more killers off the streets. Still, she had a sick feeling about this whole case, and not just because of the grotesque demise of Vincent Gianelli.

The dead had crossed decades, and her team would spend months trying to identify all them; but, in the end, their killers would not go unpunished.

"Vincent would have taken my place," Gianelli said wistfully. "Run the family . . . but like everybody who's going anywhere in the organization, he had to become a made man. That's what he did with Stewart."

Booth frowned. "Vince killed Musetti *himself*?"

"Yeah," the old man said, and his chuckle was like parchment rubbing against itself. "Even Raymond Gianelli's son has to make his bones, you know."

A NOTE FROM THE AUTHOR

I would like to thank Lieutenant Chris Kauffman, CLPE, Bettendorf Police Department, Bettendorf, IA, for his expert input; and Lieutenant Paul Van Steenhuyse, Scott County Sheriff's Department, Scott County, IA, for Patriot Act information.

Researcher/co-plotter Matthew V. Clemens wishes to acknowledge Stefan Schmitt, Florida Department of Law Enforcement, for his forensic archeology workshop at the IAI conference.

Also helpful were Michele Kuder and Mary Kay Majot from the Dorothy Buell Memorial Visitor Center, Indiana Dunes National Lakeshore, Indiana, generously sharing information about the Indiana Dunes Inland Marsh and related subjects.

I also wish to thank Kathy Reichs for sharing her anthropological expertise. And thank you to Scott Shannon for bringing us together, and to editor Jennifer Heddle; and also to the producers and writers of the Fox television series *Bones*, for sharing materials and providing inspiration.

ABOUT THE AUTHOR

Max Allan Collins was hailed in 2004 by *Publishers Weekly* as "a new breed of writer." A frequent Mystery Writers of America Edgar nominee, he has earned an unprecedented fourteen Private Eye Writers of America Shamus nominations for his historical thrillers, winning for his Nathan Heller novels, *True Detective* (1983) and *Stolen Away* (1991).

His graphic novel *Road to Perdition* is the basis of the Academy Award–winning film starring Tom Hanks, directed by Sam Mendes. His many comics credits include the syndicated strip *Dick Tracy;* his own *Ms. Tree; Batman;* and *CSI: Crime Scene Investigation*, based on the hit TV series for which he has also written video games, jigsaw puzzles, and a *USA Today*–bestselling series of novels.

An independent filmmaker, he wrote and directed the Lifetime movie *Mommy* (1996) and a 1997 sequel, *Mommy's Day*. He wrote *The Expert*, a 1995 HBO World Premiere, and wrote and directed the innovative made-for-DVD feature, "Real Time: Siege at

Lucas Street Market" (2000). "Shades of Noir" (2004), an anthology of his short films, includes his award-winning documentary, *Mike Hammer's Mickey Spillane*.

His other credits include film criticism, short fiction, songwriting, trading-card sets, and movie/TV tie-in novels, including the *New York Times* bestseller *Saving Private Ryan*. His one-man show, *Eliot Ness: An Untouchable Life*, was nominated for an Edgar for Best Play of 2004 by the Mystery Writers of America; a film version, written and directed by Collins, is currently in post-production.

Collins lives in Muscatine, Iowa, with his wife, writer Barbara Collins; and their son, Nathan. He and Barbara have collaborated on numerous short stories and several novels, sometimes writing as "Barbara Allan."

Bare Bones

Kathy Reichs

It's one of the hottest summers on record and forensic anthropologist Dr Temperance Brennan is looking forward to a long overdue vacation. But it's not to be . . .

First, the bones of a newborn baby are found in a wood stove; the mother, barely a child herself, has disappeared.

Next, a Cessna flies into a rock face. The bodies of the pilot and passenger are burned beyond recognition, and covered in an unknown substance.

And then a cache of bones is found in a remote corner of the county. But what happened there, and who will the next victim be? The answers lie hidden deep within the bones – if only Tempe can decipher them in time . . .

'The forensic detail is harrowing, the pace relentless, and the prose assured. Kathy Reichs just gets better and better and is now the Alpha female of this genre'
Irish Independent

'Reichs has now proved that she is up there with the best'
The Times

'Better than Patricia Cornwell'
Sunday Express

arrow books

Monday Mourning

Kathy Reichs

Three skeletons are found in the basement of a pizza parlour.

The building is old, with a colourful past, and Homicide Detective Luc Claudel dismisses the remains as historic. Not his case, not his concern . . .

But forensic anthropologist Tempe Brennan has her doubts. Something about the bones of the three young women suggests a different message: murder. A cold case, but Claudel's case nonetheless.

Brennan is in Montreal to testify as an expert witness at a trial. Digging up more bones was not on her agenda. And to make matters worse, her sometime-lover Detective Andrew Ryan disappears just as Tempe is beginning to trust him.

Soon Tempe finds herself drawn ever deeper into a web of evil from which there may be no escape: three women have disappeared, never to return. And Tempe may be next . . .

'Reichs is not just "as good as" Cornwell, she has become the finer writer'
Daily Express

'Terrific'
Independent on Sunday

arrow books